Triple Threat

Triple Threat

A Bella James Mystery

Alexis Koetting

IGUANA

Published by Iguana Books
720 Bathurst Street, Suite 303
Toronto, Ontario, Canada
M5S 2R4

Publisher / Editor: Mary Ann J. Blair
Front cover image: Noose by Mega Pixel/Shutterstock.com /
Grunge background by Nik Merkulov/Shutterstock.com
Author photo: Helen Tansey
Cover design: Ruth Dwight

Issued in print and electronic formats.

ISBN 978-1-77180-257-4 (paperback)
ISBN 978-1-77180-258-1 (EPUB)
ISBN 978-1-77180-259-8 (Kindle)

This is an original print edition of *Triple Threat*.

For Grady-the-Great

Alive on these pages and in my heart

A threat *is a declaration of intent to cause harm, pain, injury, or punishment. The word* triple *indicates something that consists of three parts or that occurs three times.*

In the theatre, the term triple threat *refers to someone who can sing, dance, and act.*

Chapter 1

CFA, or "come from away," is an East Coast term given to anyone not born on the East Coast. Prince Edward Island takes it one step further and bestows the moniker to anyone not born on the Island itself. It doesn't matter how long you've lived there or what great contributions you might have made to the province; if your first breath was not of island air, then a CFA you'll always be.

My parents were born and raised on PEI but moved away shortly after they were married, making me a first-generation CFA. They were killed in a car accident when I was eight and the Island that had only ever been "the place where Grandma lives" became my home. Whether it was out of pity for my orphan status or respect for my grandmother, I had no idea I came with a label. It wasn't until I started high school that my name took on the notorious post-nominal initials.

At first it was only a few whispers. Then one of the older boys came up with the idea to adapt the Styx song "Come Sail Away" to "Come from Away" and took to singing the musical refrain, *"Come from away, Come from away, So get away from me,"* whenever he was in my vicinity. I was a sullen child who grew into an even more sullen teenager. If I had allowed myself any sense of humour, I likely would have appreciated his cleverness or even recognized that the attention he was paying me was a ruse to get me to notice him rather than the cruel torment I took it to be. I knew the only reason I was on the island was because of an unspeakable loss. I blamed everyone, rejected any offerings of friendship or comfort, and saw to it that my high school years were miserable for all.

Mercifully, but by no means quickly, I outgrew my hatred of the world and everyone in it. But standing at the base of the steps of Niagara-on-the-Lake's Niagara District Secondary School, known familiarly as NDSS, I could hear the ghosts of my past start in with, *"I've come from away..."* and every fibre in my being told me to run.

"Ms. James?" A male voice called a halt to my escape.

I looked up to see a large man weaving an easy descent against a sea of oncoming students. No small feat given his size. The man was huge in every sense of the word, and when he finally reached me at the foot of the stairs, I had to shield my eyes against the sun to meet his gaze.

"Ms. James?" he asked again.

"Bella. Please."

"Gerald Harvey," he said, extending a hand that completely swallowed my own. "I'm the principal here. I'm afraid … um … I understand you were supposed to meet Al Macie."

"Yes, when I spoke with him on the phone, he said he'd meet me in front of the school."

Principal Harvey surveyed the students, nodding greetings and offering smiles. He did so with tremendous effort, however. Only an expert in pretending everything is fine when it's not would be able to pick up on it and unfortunately for him, I was one such expert.

"Mr. Harvey, is everything all right?"

He looked at me and revved up his smile. "Just a busy morning. But know we're very happy to have you here, Ms. James. Bella. This is a wonderful opportunity for our students," he said, referring to the pilot project the Shaw Festival was running in cooperation with the school.

In addition to offering world-class theatre, the Festival offered workshops to both teachers and students throughout the school year and an acting intensive during the summer. This season the Festival was trying out an Artist-in-the-Classroom program as a possible extension of its already successful education series. Company members in various disciplines—design, acting, dance, and directing—would work in the classroom alongside a teacher at the school as a means of enhancing the arts program. I'd been paired with Al Macie.

"Mr. Macie told me his students are very excited. I'm looking forward to meeting them," I said as convincingly as possible.

If truth be told, I had come aboard this project kicking and screaming. I was in no rush to relive any of the high school experience, even if I had some semblance of authority behind me this time. Then there was the question of scheduling. Unlike my previous season at the Festival where I had opened my first show before my second even went into rehearsal, this season had me rehearsing two shows simultaneously. The addition of two mornings every week at the school for an eight-week period had sent me into a full-on panic.

"Yes, the students are thrilled about having Emma Samuel as one of their mentors," Principal Harvey said.

"I should have guessed," I said, laughing.

Detective Emma Samuel was a role I'd played on the TV series *Port Authority* for many years and, in spite of the critical acclaim I had garnered on stage at the Shaw

Festival during the previous season, everyone saw Detective Samuel when they looked at me.

An awkward silence fell over us.

"So, shall I wait here for Mr. Macie or—"

"Ms. James, we've had a little … um … There's been… Perhaps you'd just better come with me."

Chapter 2

"Have a seat," Gerald Harvey said, ushering me into his office and closing the door.

I settled in one of two chairs facing the desk while he circled around to stand on the other side, taking a handkerchief from his pocket and wiping his forehead en route. Although we had been walking quickly and while it was true that the man was likely morbidly obese by definition, I didn't think the sweat forming on his brow was from overexertion.

"Mr. Harvey," I began tentatively.

A knock on the door cut me off.

"I'm sorry to interrupt," a tall, slender blonde said, as she poked her head in. She glanced at me and waited for permission to continue in my presence. Gerald Harvey gave a nod and she went on, "The police have arrived. I've asked them to wait outside until the bell. I figured the fewer students lingering the better."

"Yes, absolutely," Harvey said, bringing the handkerchief into action again as new beads of sweat formed.

"I told them you'd be right out," she said, sympathetically.

"Thank you, Donna." The woman made no move to go. "Is there something else?"

"I've gone ahead and covered Al's first class. Cynthia's taking it."

Harvey nodded then caught himself. "She's not—"

"No," Donna said, anticipating his question. "She's taking them into the cafeteria."

"Fine. Good."

My ears pricked up at the mention of "Al," who I assumed to be Al Macie.

"Do you want me to see if I can find someone to cover the rest of the day?" Donna asked.

"I don't think that'll be necessary."

Donna smiled sadly and made her exit.

Gerald Harvey tucked the handkerchief into the breast pocket of his suit jacket and jammed his hands into the pockets of his pants. His eyes focused on the floor for a few moments before looking to me.

"Ms. James," he started, "Al Macie committed suicide. Here, at the school. His body was found first thing this morning."

"Oh my god."

My mind whirled back to the conversation I'd had with Al earlier in the week. He had talked of his students' excitement about meeting me and I got the feeling he was using theirs to disguise some of his own. He'd been passionate about his class and enthusiastic about our partnership. I remember thinking right away I was going to like him.

"I'm so sorry," I said, through my shock.

Harvey nodded his thanks.

"I'm sure we'll be able to make other arrangements for you, but for the moment…"

"Of course," I said, standing, fully aware he had already spent more time with me than necessary and was needed elsewhere. A zillion elsewheres, I imagined.

"If you'll excuse me," he said.

I watched Principal Harvey walk heavily out of his office and out into the main hallway of the school where he stopped to receive some good-natured ribbing from a couple of boys about the loss of some sporting event. I admired how, for even a few minutes more, he was trying to give his students the normal day they had expected when they'd woken up.

I hadn't paid attention during the walk to Harvey's office and, as a result, found myself wandering the maze that was the high school looking for an exit. As I passed a series of open lockers, my nostrils twitched against the onslaught of sweaty gym socks, pubescent B.O., and teenage angst. I heard the morning announcements ask students to please clear the hallways, as the police would be conducting random locker searches during the first period. This sent a groan and a few choice words rippling down the corridor. I knew small amounts of marijuana were, at that precise moment, being furiously moved from one hiding place to another to avoid detection, and I suppressed a smile. I also knew if the police were hoping to remove Al Macie's body discreetly they'd have to come up with something better than a locker search.

As if reading my mind, the voice on the PA system added, "And there will be an assembly in the auditorium during period two. Attendance by all students and staff is mandatory."

Another groan.

An exit came into view just as the national anthem started to play. I stood dutifully at attention while students fidgeted around me and staff members stared at the floor with glazed eyes. I imagined many of Al Macie's colleagues had only had a chance to take a few sips of their morning coffees before hearing the news of his death, which alone would have come as a shock. The details of his demise would have made the news particularly hard to digest.

The song was in its final verse when a flutter of the blinds in the window next to where I was standing caught my attention. Through the slats I could see a young female student, visibly shaken, sitting alone in an office. She had a wad of tissues in her hand and an empty Kleenex box in her lap. Her red eyes met mine for a brief moment before a stern looking woman entered the office with tissue reinforcements and clicked the blinds closed. Movement in the hall resumed as the anthem played its final chords and, taking my cue from the students, I inched closer to the exit, anxious to take advantage of the few unexpected free hours that had just opened up in my schedule.

My descent down the steps of the school was met by a wolf whistle. I rolled my eyes in the direction of the sound and was just in time to catch the culprit in the act of removing his fingers from his mouth.

"Does your wife know you go around whistling at women?" I asked a smiling Detective Sergeant Andre Jeffers.

"How do you think I got her attention in the first place?"

Detective Jeffers was one of the six detective sergeants that made up the Homicide division of the Niagara Regional Police's Major Crime Unit. He was also one of my best friends.

"What are you doing here?" I asked, joining Jeffers across the street from the school where he was waiting along with the team from the coroner's office and a number of uniformed police officers. Gerald Harvey was among them, speaking into a walkie-talkie. He took little notice of me. There was not a sniffer dog in sight, which would have tipped off any student with the most average of GPAs that the so-called locker search was a crock.

"The principal told me it was a suicide," I said.

"Any and all dead bodies come to us," Jeffers said. "You should know that, Samuel. Didn't they teach you anything on that show?" He winked.

Ever since our meeting, more than a year before, Jeffers had taken to calling me by the name of my TV personality and often assumed because I had played a detective on television, I knew all the ins and outs of the business.

"They taught us locker searches usually have dogs," I countered.

"Touché."

"Besides, we never had any suicides on the show," I said, furthering my defence.

"In seven years?"

I shrugged.

"Shoddy," Jeffers scoffed.

"I didn't write it!"

"Anyway," he said, "the bigger question is, what are *you* doing here?"

I gave Jeffers the Coles Notes version of what was to have been my collaboration with the victim.

"You knew him?" he asked.

"We'd only talked on the phone."

"And?"

"Seemed nice enough. Said he and the students were excited to meet me. Told me he had a lot of great stuff planned ... I don't know what else I can tell you."

"Hmmm."

"What?"

Jeffers opened his mouth to speak but was interrupted by Harvey, who announced he could take the group inside now.

"Have fun," I said, and turned to go.

"Walk with me," Jeffers said, falling in step behind two paramedics pushing a gurney.

"What? I can't!"

"Sure you can. You were supposed to be here anyway. What else have you got to do?"

I rolled my eyes. One of the shows I was rehearsing was a musical—the first musical of my professional career and only the second in my lifetime. I was scared to death. Any spare minute I had was spent reviewing choreography, going through vocal exercises assigned by the singing coach, and doing anything and everything to keep from looking a complete idiot in time for the first audience.

"You don't know the half. And besides, Inspector Morris—"

Jeffers cut me off with a snicker.

I had first made the acquaintance of Inspector Roger Morris a little over a year ago after an unsanctioned investigation Jeffers and I had been running had become too big for us and we were forced to confess our actions to the man in charge. While Jeffers had been allowed to continue with the case, my involvement had been permitted only after being granted a special dispensation. A dispensation Morris had been very clear to point out was a one-time thing.

In the end, Jeffers had been suspended for five months while waiting out a divisional review of his actions and I had almost died in our efforts to uncover the truth. In spite of the fact that we had successfully closed the case, I doubted Morris would look favourably on another such pairing.

"Let me worry about Morris," Jeffers said.

"Jeffers, I—"

"Come on," he said, smiling, "It'll be fun! It'll be just like old times."

"That's what I'm afraid of."

Al Macie's body was hanging from one of the pipes that made up the lighting grid in a small, studio theatre. A tall stool lay on its side under his feet. I had never seen a hanging victim before and was surprised by how peaceful Mr. Macie looked. If it hadn't been for the smallest protrusion of a swollen purple tongue, I would not have been surprised to see his hands come up to release the grip the electrical cord had around his neck and proudly begin a lesson in special effects.

He had a nice face, and I thought how well it matched his voice. His dark goatee lent an air of mystery to his otherwise gentle features. There was a warmth about him. Even in death.

The uniforms immediately began securing the room while the coroner's team began their set up. One of the officers took out a camera and wasted no time photographing the scene. By the time Jeffers had properly donned his plastic gloves and booties, the officer had finished taking preliminaries of the body and had ordered a ladder brought in so he could turn his attention to the makeshift noose.

I refused Jeffers' offer of plastic gloves and chose to remain firmly in the doorway of the room. I didn't know what Jedi mind trick he was planning to use on Morris to explain my presence at the scene, so I wanted to stay as far away from the action as possible. Gerald Harvey stood next to me systematically dabbing his forehead, checking his watch, and looking nervously up and down the empty hallway.

"Detective Jeffers said you've worked with the police before?" Harvey asked. "Was it Victim Services or something?"

"Something like that, yes," I said, understanding why the principal didn't seem to question my being there.

I'd worked with Jeffers closely enough to know I was not there because of my charming disposition and sense of humour. Jeffers hoped I'd be able to learn something about the victim by talking to Harvey. People don't like talking to the police if they can help it. They tend to divulge more than they realize when they believe the conversation isn't an official one.

"Mr. Harvey, did Al Macie ever—"

My question was interrupted by the voice of the coroner. "I need everyone to stop moving right now!" she said. "Detective Jeffers, if you'll join me?"

Jeffers walked carefully over to her and together they looked up at Macie's body.

"Typically in a hanging of this nature, ligature marks present as upward-pointing V-shaped bruising. The upward direction shows that the ligature, the cord in this instance, was countering the pull of gravity."

"But there is no bruising." Jeffers said. "Oh, god, you're not telling me…"

The coroner gave a slight nod and Jeffers' shoulders slumped.

"I'll know more when I get the body back to the lab, but I can tell you in absolute certainty this man was dead before that cord went around his neck."

Jeffers exhaled loudly and ran his fingers through his hair. "All right, people, you heard her. We've got ourselves a crime scene."

Chapter 3

I convinced Jeffers to excuse me once the case became a murder investigation. I knew Inspector Morris would have both our hides if he heard I was even within one hundred feet of the scene. This left me with one precious, unexpected hour before I was due at rehearsal.

I was singing one particularly difficult bit of harmony as I walked through the door of my cottage and narrowly avoided an object hurtling toward my head.

The sight before me was like one of those cartoon moments when everything is briefly frozen in time and the characters think they're invisible. I took the blur of beige and fur to be my dear dog, Moustache, thirty pounds of something crossed with a poodle. He was in mid-leap off the landing of the staircase in the hall and his veterinarian, Dr. Gorgeous, was mid-barrel down the steps behind him. The nickname had been affectionately bestowed on the vet by my libido when we first met more than a couple of moons ago. Both dog and doctor had stupid grins on their faces, knowing they'd been caught in the act but hoping I wouldn't notice.

"What are you doing here?" I asked, as action resumed.

Moustache slid into the front door and grabbed the stuffed lion that had almost decapitated me. He gave a triumphant snort in Dr. Gorgeous' direction and ran into the living room. The good doctor at least had the decency to acknowledge my presence.

"I thought you weren't coming back till later," he said and planted a kiss on my cheek.

"And I thought you had a surgery this morning."

"I did, but once we got the little guy on the table, we found there wasn't any necrosis in the intestines after all. That's good news in case you were wondering. That also meant the procedure took half the time. My next appointment wasn't for a while so I figured I could either get caught up on some paperwork or get in some exercise."

"In the form of fetch with Moustache?"

"Well, had I known you were going to be here, I would have come over with something entirely different in mind," he said, taking me in his arms and kissing me deeply.

An approving woof emanated from the living room. Moustache liked to take all the credit for getting us together.

It was a chance run-in with the dog that had left Dr. Gorgeous sitting in a mud puddle. I'd been mortified and begged to make amends. Dr. Gorgeous had insisted I take him for a drink. The drink led to dinner, and the dinner to ten months later. The first time he kissed me I had been rambling on about something not at all important, trying to avoid the inevitable clumsiness that always accompanies the end of a first date and, in doing so, making it even more awkward. He finally took my face in his hands and stopped me mid-sentence by bringing his mouth to my own. My knees had weakened then and did so still.

"So how was it playing teacher? Were the students all suitably impressed?" he asked.

I gave him the rundown of my morning. His hold around my waist loosened.

"What?" I asked.

"Look, I know it's not my place," he said, "but I … I don't want you involved in this. Not again."

"I'm not involved."

"Bells, Jeffers brought you to the see the body!"

"Only because he thought it was a suicide. As soon as he knew it was a murder, I left."

"What difference does that make? Suicide. Murder. You're not a cop."

"I know that," I said.

"I just … I don't want you to get hurt."

The last case I had helped Jeffers with had ended up with me being rushed to hospital and Moustache, to Dr. Gorgeous. Although he knew some of what had happened, it was not until we were several months into our relationship that I finally opened up to him about the whole story.

"I'm not involved," I repeated gently. I took his hands in mine and stared into the green of his eyes.

"You say that now," he said, a smile warming his skepticism.

"How much time do you have before your next appointment?"

"I still have a few minutes."

"In that case, I'd rather not spend it arguing a moot point."

His arms went back around my waist. "Why, Ms. James. What did you have in mind?"

I walked into rehearsal to find my understudy working through one of my scenes with the leading man. Granted, they were off in a corner of the rehearsal hall, away from where the choreographer was finishing up one of the dance numbers, but it still irked me.

Manda Rogers had enjoyed leading roles in several of the Festival's previous musicals. When *Cabaret* was announced as part of this season, everyone, including Manda, figured she was a shoo-in for the role of Sally Bowles. Although I didn't witness it, I'd heard she'd thrown a tantrum of epic proportions when she got the news the role had been offered to me. To add insult to injury, she had been contracted to understudy my Sally and play the role of Fräulein Kost, a woman moved to "entertain" the sailors in order to survive in 1930s Berlin. The role was written such that Manda could potentially steal any scene she was in if she could just get over her jealousy and focus on her own part rather than mine.

She caught my eye, ran her fingers through her gorgeous red mane, and turned her performance up a notch. Powell Avery, the man playing Cliff to my Sally, mouthed an apology to me and rolled his eyes as Manda sashayed around him. I gave him a wink and moved to the opposite corner of the room.

"God, that woman is shameless," Adam Lange said, plopping down next to me.

Adam was one of the first people I met when I started at the Festival the year before. His flamboyant exuberance had eased my first-day jitters and we'd become fast friends.

"You're the bad guy in all of this," I said. "I don't know why she doesn't hate *you*. If you hadn't talked me into doing that *Rocky Horror* send up at the SNAG, Roberta never would have heard me sing and come up with the insane idea of giving me this part in the first place. And I wasn't even that good!"

On certain Saturday nights during the season there are open mic performances in the basement of the Royal George Theatre, thus the acronym SNAG standing for "Saturday

Nights at the George." Adam had roped a group of us into doing a silly performance during one of these and I just so happened to catch the attention of the Festival's artistic director, Roberta Hayward.

"Don't sell yourself short, sister. And besides, Sally isn't supposed to be a great singer."

"Thanks a lot."

"You know what I mean."

I did. And even though the role terrified me, I had to admit I found the challenge incredibly exhilarating. She was a kind of character I'd never played before: eccentric, charming, yet totally unapologetic about using people to serve her own needs. Sally's approach to life is seemingly unaffected by what's happening around her. Her world is simply her. Even when met with tragedy or hardship, she appears relatively unscathed. There was something in her ability to pick herself up and dust herself off that I admired. Envied even.

My eye turned to Manda again. She might be able to sing circles around me, but she was nowhere near the actress she needed to be to pull off this role. No matter how often she dragged poor Powell into a corner.

Adam caught me watching. "I don't think she wants to run the scene as much as she wants to run her hands all over Powell," he said. "And to be quite honest, who wouldn't."

"Down boy."

Manda was notorious for her sexual escapades and had wielded the final blow to many a marriage.

"It doesn't look like he's buying," I said, and inwardly applauded Powell's resistance.

I liked Powell. And I liked working with him. I was happy to see he was smart enough not to be sucked in by

Manda's charms. Adam looked at me and cocked an eyebrow.

"What?" I asked.

"Are you kidding me? The only female Powell's interested in petting is his cat."

My jaw dropped.

"You look surprised."

"I am," I admitted. "He's never struck me as—"

"I know. But that boy's got 'man' written all over him," Adam said lustfully.

We both took a moment to admire the view.

"You ever think of asking him out?" I asked.

"Look at him! Totally out of my league."

"And when has that ever stopped you before?"

"True," he said with a wink and moved toward Powell, who now had Manda on his lap. "But first I'm going to get into his good graces by saving him from that insatiable siren."

There were two messages on my voice mail when I got out of rehearsal. One, I was expecting. The other stopped me in my tracks.

Chapter 4

"Bella, this is Maureen from the education department at the Festival. Terrible what happened to Al Macie. We're all in shock over here. Anyway, just so you know, the school has cancelled classes for the rest of the week while the police investigate and the grief counsellors are arranged. But they do want to go ahead with the program as planned. There is another teacher coming in to take over Al's classes. His name is Vincent Leduc. I've given him your number and I expect he'll be in touch sooner rather than later. So sorry about all this but who could ever have imagined? If you have any questions, you know where I am. Bye for now."

I hadn't really expected the Artist-in-the-Classroom program to have been sacked completely, but part of me had been secretly hoping for a little less time in the classroom and a little more time in rehearsal. Things being what they were, I crossed my fingers that Vincent Leduc was as nice and as enthusiastic about working together as Al Macie had been. I erased the message and the system went on to the next.

"Ms. James. Roger Morris here from the Niagara Regional Police. I understand there's no need to catch you up on the details of this morning's events."

I braced myself for a reprimand. I knew it wouldn't be explosive as that wasn't Morris' style. He preferred the calm, understated approach that, in my experience, made him more terrifying.

The message continued. "Sergeant Jeffers has filled me in on your involvement with the school and thinks you may be of use to us as far as this investigation is concerned. I am reluctant to agree with him, as I'm sure you can imagine, but I will admit Sergeant Jeffers has made some valid points and I'm willing to permit your participation … for the time being. He'll fill you in on the details. I will remind you that your association with this case does not afford you any protection by the system and that you have no special authority whatsoever. And Ms. James," he paused for what seemed like an eternity, "I trust I don't need to advise you to exercise caution at all times."

There was no goodbye. Just the warning.

"What'd I tell you about Morris? We're back in business." Jeffers sat on my front steps wearing a triumphant grin.

"I have to hand it to you," I said. "You've accomplished the impossible."

"Morris is a piece of cake."

"Don't let him hear you say that. He said you'd fill me in on the details."

"That, Detective Samuel, is why I'm here. And to sweeten the deal, I've got my wife's famous gnocchi and a bottle of so-so wine."

"How does Aria have time to cook with a seven-month-old?"

"Because our son is perfect. The only child I've ever known who actually sleeps when we want him to."

"That's not going to last, you know."

"I know. But until that day comes, Aria and I are content to be the two most rested new parents in the world. And the best fed. Let's get this gnocchi in the oven and get down to business."

"No Doc tonight?" Jeffers asked from the living room while I plated the food in the kitchen.

"He's got a conference call in an hour or so and an early surgery tomorrow."

"You guys thinking about moving in together?"

"It's only been ten months."

"So?"

"So?" I said, joining Jeffers on the couch and handing him a steaming plate. "This is the first decent relationship I've had in ages. I'm not going to screw it all up by rushing things. It's enough that we've exchanged keys."

"I'm only bringing it up because he seems to be here an awful lot."

"Can we talk about something else?"

"I'm just saying—"

"Tell me what you know about Al Macie," I said, cutting off any further scrutiny of my love life.

"Okay, according to the preliminary tests, it appears he was killed between six and seven this morning," Jeffers said around a mouthful of pasta.

"That's awfully early to be at the school," I said.

"I agree. It's possible he was lured there by his killer."

Moustache came galloping into the living room, still chewing the last of his own dinner but not wanting to miss any chance at sampling some of ours. He sat at our feet looking from me to Jeffers and back again.

"So if he didn't die by hanging, do we know how he died?" I asked.

"Crushed windpipe. The coroner's ruling it a manual strangulation."

"But wouldn't there be imprints from the hands?" I asked.

"Not if it was a chokehold of some kind. In Macie's case, it's likely there was significant pressure on the neck from a forearm. That's why there's very little external evidence. The coroner said it could be hours, even days, before bruising presents. If at all. We're hoping for some marks that might result in a pattern, a shape, anything that might give us a clue as to what the killer was wearing."

"Would it have been quick? His death?"

"Typically in cases like this the victim dies within minutes. He would have experienced severe pain before losing consciousness, and he would have been brain dead before death took hold."

"What a terrible way to die."

I hadn't known Al Macie, but the feeling I got from him in our few exchanges was that he was a good man. I hated that he had suffered. I sighed and put my unfinished gnocchi on the coffee table. Moustache made a few unsuccessful attempts to reach the plate before giving up and turning his attention back to Jeffers.

"This kind of strangling indicates the killer would have been bigger than Macie. Not in height, but in brawn," Jeffers explained. "It requires a tremendous amount of strength. If they'd been physically matched, Macie would have easily been able to fight off his attacker."

"So likely a man."

Jeffers nodded. "Pretty strongly built."

My mind flickered to the only image I had of him. Hanging from a pipe. He'd had height to his credit but had been very slim and finely boned. A man with any muscle could have easily overpowered him.

"When was his body found?"

"About seven thirty."

"Wow! That's a short window in which to stage a suicide."

"Which gives me reason to believe it was someone familiar with the school."

"And, therefore, someone he knew."

"Yep."

"God," I said, shaking my head. "That's a long list."

"And that's where you come in. We need you to keep your eyes and ears open for anything people might not want to share with the police."

"And you think they're going to open up to me?"

"You're Emma Samuel," Jeffers said. "Everyone loves getting close to a celebrity." I rolled my eyes. "It's true. You'll see. All you need to do is get people talking. They'll let their guard down sooner with you than they will with us."

"I'm not so sure about that, but I'll do what I can. Anybody in particular you want me to seek out?"

"Elsbeth Penner. Seventeen-year-old student who found Macie. She was in considerable shock when I spoke with her and didn't say much. Her father was with her and he struck me as a tad overprotective. I doubt I'll get a chance to interview her alone."

"Can you give me a description so I know who I'm looking for?"

"She's Mennonite. She dresses traditionally. Long dress. Cap. It's a big community around here."

My mind flashed to the girl I had seen crying at the school. "Okay. Anyone else?"

"Like you said, Samuel, it's a long list."

Chapter 5

News of Al Macie's murder rocked the town. Niagara-on-the-Lake is small. It's a town that has been founded on generation upon generation; if you look through the phone book, you'll see dozens of Klassens, Enns, and Janzens, to name a few. It is not so small that everyone knows your name or your business, but every face is familiar and what business needs to be known, is.

To say that nothing happens in Niagara-on-the-Lake would be far from the truth. As one of its newer residents, I'd learned the town had long enjoyed the reputation as one of the prettiest in Canada. It boasts world-famous wineries and is an area rich in history, having been Canada's first capital as well as home to the country's first library, newspaper, post office, bank, and courthouse. It is an extremely popular destination for tourists from all over the world. Whether they come for the wine, the history, or the theatre, the steady flow of traffic in and out of the town has become as well known a fixture as its clock tower on Queen Street and its gazebo overlooking Lake Ontario. Something was always happening in Niagara-on-the-Lake, but usually nothing bad.

A pall lingered over the town in the days following the murder, but it was thickest at the high school. I'd been invited to meet Vincent Leduc at the school early Friday morning to discuss our plans for when classes resumed. A small handful of staff moved zombielike through their business as I made my way to Al Macie's office. The door was ajar when I got there.

"Hello," I said, sticking my head around the open door.

"Oh, God, you scared me," a man said, clutching his chest and whirling around to face me.

"I'm sorry. I should have knocked."

"No. It's fine. I just didn't expect anyone would be coming in here."

When I had spoken with Vincent Leduc, I was certain this was where he had suggested we meet. I opened my mouth to voice my confusion.

"You're Bella James," the man said before I could speak.

"Yes, I—"

"You're just as pretty in real life."

"Uh, thank you," I said, feeling colour rising in my cheeks. "I hope I'm not late. I know you said eight thirty, but—"

"I'm sorry?"

"We were supposed to go over plans for—"

"Ah. You're meeting someone. I won't be long. I'm Glynn." He said the name like it was supposed to mean something. I shook my head. "Glynn Radley," he repeated. "Al's partner."

He was tall and thin. Just like Al Macie had been. But with a little more muscle.

"I came by to pick up some of his things," he went on. "I should have come by sooner but I couldn't bring myself..."

"Of course. I'm so sorry for your loss."

"I'm, uh…" he stammered, his eyes starting to well. "He was very excited to be working with you. I was so jealous. I told him to be sure to get all the *Port Authority* scoop. I'd made up a dozen excuses to come by the class so I could meet you. I guess now … This wasn't the way I pictured it."

Jeffers had been right after all about people wanting to cozy up to a celebrity. Time to keep up my end of the bargain. "Mr. Radley—"

"Glynn, please."

"Glynn. I'm sorry I never got a chance to meet Al. He seemed lovely over the phone."

"Lovely. That really is the perfect word to describe him," he said sadly. "We were together for twenty-one years and I never once heard him say a bad word about anybody. Can you believe that? In twenty-one years?" I smiled and let him continue. "Bully directors, angry parents, difficult colleagues, even bad waiters. They all got a pass when it came to Al. It's one of the things I loved most about him. Always seeing the good. But it drove me crazy too, you know? Sometimes I just wanted him to lash out. To yell at the top of his lungs. Throw something. I mean he must have felt … frustrated. Angry. At times. Where does that all go?"

"I—"

"I'm sorry. God, listen to me."

"It's fine," I said, smiling reassuringly. "It's important for you to talk through things. Especially at a time like this. Believe me. I learned that lesson the hard way."

"I'm trying, you know?" Glynn said, tears coming to his eyes and his voice catching. "I'm really trying to understand how somebody … I know Al would want me to forgive, but…"

"From what you've told me about him, I can't believe Al would have had any enemies."

"Oh, I didn't say that. Al may have seen the good in everyone, but that doesn't mean—"

"I'm so sorry I'm late," a man said, rushing down the hall toward me. "I had to fill out some forms in the office in order to ... Glynn."

"Vince?"

I'd been standing close to the door and had been visible from the hall but it wasn't until Vincent Leduc turned into the office that he saw I wasn't alone. The two men stared at one another.

"I don't believe this," Glynn said, clocking the box of personal belongings Vincent carried. "You didn't waste any time, did you?"

"Glynn, this wasn't my decision," Vincent said calmly. "The board asked—"

"Yeah," Glynn retorted, "sure it did." He grabbed the box containing Al's things and walked out of the room.

I stood, frozen, unsure whether I should speak. Vincent Leduc had his back to me and he sighed heavily as he placed his box on the desk. Finally he turned to face me.

"Bella," he said, extending his hand. "Vincent Leduc. Call me Vince."

"Nice to meet you, Vince."

"I'm sorry about all that."

"Not at all," I said, dying to know what "all that" was. "Glynn seemed upset to learn you're taking over Al's class."

"He'll get over it," he said with a bit of a chuckle.

"You know them well? Glynn and Al?"

"Mostly Al. Listen, can I get you a coffee or something before we start?"

"I'm fine."

"Give me five minutes?"

"Of course."

He took a mug out of the box and left me alone in the office.

I could see a copy of Sanford Meisner's book, *On Acting*, among Vince's things and I reached for it without thinking. Meisner's teachings were legendary and his book can be found on the shelves of almost every actor. During my first year of theatre school I'd had a teacher who had studied with him and had implemented his technique in our class. I flipped through the pages of the book, shaking my head at the memory of the Repetition Exercise, which had been the bane of my existence. One of my flips sent a photograph falling to the floor.

A group of men were standing on the steps of a building I didn't recognize. Their arms were linked and they appeared to be on the descent. I recognized a much younger Al Macie at one end of the line. He looked to be in mid-laugh. In fact all of the men appeared to be having a great time. All but one. A man at the other end of the line who I was sure was Vincent Leduc.

"This photo is key," I said over the phone to Jeffers later that night. "There's more to both Glynn and Al's relationships with Vince. Vince clearly didn't want to discuss it. Hopefully Glynn will be more forthcoming. I've already called him and asked if we could meet."

"Look at Samuel, showing initiative. What's your plan?"

"Glynn was at the school picking up some of Al's personal effects. I told him I found this photograph and thought he might like to have it. I said it was in one of Al's books. If he doesn't want it, I'll sneak it back into the office. It's a way to get the conversation started."

"OK. Did either of them know anything about Elsbeth?"

"It didn't occur to me to ask."

"Damn."

"Why don't you just go talk to her? She's the one who found Al's body. She's pretty material to the case. It only makes sense the police would need to speak to her."

"I did. This morning. Her father kept a pretty tight leash on the situation. The best I could get was that she was at the school to meet a friend to study."

"At seven in the morning?"

"Apparently she had a big test that afternoon."

"But you don't believe her?"

"No. I know if I could talk to her without her father looming over us she'd have more to say. And when I say 'I', I mean you."

"I'll do my best," I said. "Classes resume next week. I'll try to get her alone."

"Don't try. Just do it."

"Yes, sir."

"Sorry."

"Jeffers, what exactly do you think she knows? She said she was at the school early to meet a friend to study and found Al's body. Why are you so sure there's more to her story?"

"Why was she in the studio?"

"Maybe she was just walking by."

"Maybe. Maybe she heard something. Maybe she saw something. Maybe the killer saw her and threatened her. I don't know. But there's more. I can just feel it."

"Did you ask any of the staff about her when you were conducting interviews?"

"I got nothing. She's a good student. Quiet. Hangs with a small group of girls. Blah blah."

"And what about Al?"

"Highly respected. A gifted teacher by all accounts. Generally well liked."

"Generally?"

"I got the feeling not all of the staff was completely comfortable with his homosexuality. But that's not surprising. And certainly no reason to kill him. Listen, when are you planning on seeing Glynn?"

"Sunday."

"Would you mind if I tagged along? When I spoke to him on the day of the murder he was understandably upset. He'd been out of town and rushed back when he got the news. He answered my questions as best he could, but now that a few days have passed, he might be able to recall something else."

"About Elsbeth?"

"Among other things."

Jeffers and I spoke for a few more minutes before hanging up.

"I thought you weren't getting involved," Dr. Gorgeous said from the doorway of the kitchen. He was drying a plate.

"You know I have a dishwasher," I said, smiling.

"Call me old fashioned. More wine?" he asked, nodding toward my empty glass.

"Thanks. And for the record," I said, as he disappeared into the kitchen, "I'm not involved. I'm just helping."

"Uh-huh."

Chapter 6

Although I refused to admit involvement in the case, I did finally confess that the recent meeting of Glynn Radley and Vincent Leduc had greatly piqued my curiosity. Not to mention Jeffers' fascination with Elsbeth Penner. His hunches were rarely wrong. Whatever intrigue I sensed in the case, however, had to be put on hold as intrigue of a political nature took focus the following afternoon.

George Bernard Shaw's play *On the Rocks* centres on an uninspiring British prime minister who finds himself increasingly more depressed and exhausted as his country's unemployed take to the streets in protest. In this season's production of the play, I was cast as The Lady, a mysterious woman who convinces the PM to take a spiritual retreat of sorts that brings about his rejuvenation and leads him to pursue wholesale nationalization. The character has only one scene, albeit a long one, near the end of the first act.

It's a two-person scene and one that I was, initially, quite excited about when I was offered the role. However, it turned out that the actor playing the prime minister was a bit of an Eeyore, a real glass half-empty kind of guy, which left me wanting to go straight from rehearsal into a therapy session.

"Oh my god," I said, as I entered Dr. Gorgeous' living room and collapsed onto his sofa. Moustache darted into the kitchen before I even had the chance to detach his leash.

"I thought you had a short day today?" Gorgeous called from the kitchen.

"I did. It's not that. It's Robert Cole. He sucks the life out of me." Moustache appeared, leash free and licking his chops. "Smells good in here."

We had started taking turns cooking dinner. Whoever's day ended first did the cooking and the other got the pleasure of cleaning up. Although my day had been relatively short, the animal hospital closed at noon on Saturdays, which made the good doctor the regular Saturday night chef.

"I'm trying something new," he called from the kitchen.

"Moustache seems to like it." The dog's tongue was still in motion.

"And he didn't even get the good stuff."

"I'm guessing there's pasta involved." I said, as a closer examination of Moustache's snout revealed a noodle stuck in his fur.

I freed the noodle and nearly lost a finger when Moustache went for it. Then I reluctantly peeled myself off the sofa and went to the kitchen to kiss the cook.

An hour and a half later, we had all but devoured a delicious rabbit ragout. Moustache, having eaten a veterinarian-approved portion, was asleep on the sofa with his full belly aimed at the sky.

"This is going to sound random, but do you know anything about the Mennonite faith?" I asked, clearing the plates.

"A little. My best friend growing up was Mennonite. Daniel Muir." He started to laugh. "I used to call him Dan Manure. He hated that. He'd get so mad."

"That's awful. I thought you said you were friends."

"We were. One day, instead of Paul Barrett, he called me Paul Bearshit. We were inseparable after that. I think that was the only time he ever swore."

"Boys and their toilet humour," I said, filling the sink with soapy water.

"Always funny. Anyway, from what I learned from Dan Manure, Mennonites are Christians following the teachings in the New Testament. I know there are some Mennonites, even around here, who are pretty conservative: living on farms, growing and raising most of their own food, using limited technology, that kind of thing. Dan's family was more modern, I guess you could say. I know there is a big focus on family and community. And they don't believe in violence as a means to an end. Dan wouldn't even play with my G.I. Joes. What's with the sudden interest?"

I told him about Elsbeth and Jeffers' asking me to talk to her alone.

"It sounds to me the issue here is an overprotective father. A person can have one of those regardless of their religion."

"True. I just didn't know if specific gender roles or anything like that might be in play in the more traditional homes."

"That I don't know. Dan was one of seven boys."

At that moment the cat flap lifted and Paul's golden-haired Maine Coon emerged. We froze and followed the cat's every move with silent eyes. I snuck a peek at where Moustache was sleeping and was relieved to find him still in the throes of his post-meal fatigue. The first time

Moustache and the cat met had resulted in a swat so violent that Moustache would have required stitches had the fur on his face not been as bushy as it was. Although relatively unhurt, the hit was enough to yield a yelp from the dog before he ran to cower behind me.

Brimstone was the meanest cat I'd ever known. All action stopped whenever he chose to present himself for fear of upsetting him and, thereby, losing a layer of skin or worse. Fortunately he spent most of his time outdoors, returning home only for meals or if it rained. He sat now at his dish eating hungrily. I looked at Paul and made a face. He smiled and threw up his hands. For whatever reason he loved that cat and happily put up with its evil ways. When the dish was empty, Brimstone cleaned himself, stretched, and disappeared through the same door that had admitted him.

"How old did you say he was?" I asked, resuming the dishwashing.

"Not sure exactly. Close to eleven."

"And cats live for how long?"

He laughed and kissed me lightly on the back of my neck. "You up for a movie?"

"Sure. Nothing with death." I had a feeling I'd get my fill of that in the coming days.

Chapter 7

I met Jeffers outside Glynn and Al's house in St. David's, a small village that retained its original name despite having been part of the Niagara-on-the-Lake Township for decades. A series of woofs answered Jeffers' knock on the door of a converted farmhouse. After a moment the barking subsided and the door opened.

"Bella, please—Detective Jeffers?" Glynn Radley had obviously been crying. "I'm sorry, I didn't realize you two—"

"No, I'm sorry," I said. "Detective Jeffers and I have worked together in the past. When I told him I was coming by he asked if he could join me. I should have checked with you to see if that was okay."

"It's fine. Of course. You're both welcome. Come in."

An enormous Great Dane came to greet us.

"This is Roger," Glynn said, taking the huge dog by the collar and leading him away into the living room where another one, only slightly smaller, was curled up on a cushion on the floor. "And this is Edith." He bent down and stroked her sleek head gently. "She's taking Al's death really hard." He indicated that we should sit. "Can I get you anything? Coffee? Water?"

"No, we're fine," Jeffers said.

"So, the fact that you're here too, Detective, does that mean there's been a lead? Have you found something?"

"Unfortunately, no," Jeffers said, and new tears sprang to Glynn's eyes. "Mr. Radley, I assure you, we are doing everything we can." Glynn nodded. Jeffers went on. "I know you answered many of these questions when we first met but sometimes it's helpful to revisit them. I'd like to try that today. Often the initial shock can cloud the mind and now that some time has passed there's a chance you'll be able to access more information."

"I'm not sure I know more now than I did then, but go ahead."

"You said you were out of town when you got the news?"

"Yes, I'm a firefighter in Toronto. We work twenty-four hour shifts. Gerald Harvey called me just before eight that morning. Told me what happened."

"Do you have any idea why Al would have been at the school so early? He must have been there before six."

Glynn nodded. "He was redesigning the drama AQ courses. The courses teachers take for additional qualifications. He had to get it done by next week and his laptop was acting up so he'd been going in to the school early and staying late to work on his computer there."

"How long had he been doing that?"

"A couple of weeks I guess."

"Did anyone else know he was at the school outside of regular hours?"

Glynn shrugged. "I suppose any one of the staff."

"Mr. Radley, I need you to think very carefully about anything that may have been troubling Al recently. Had he received any threats? Had he had any arguments with anyone?"

Glynn closed his eyes and took several moments before shaking his head.

"What about Vince?" I asked. A look of disgust flashed across Glynn's face. "I couldn't help but pick up on some tension when I was with you both in Al's office."

"Al always laughed it off, but I think Vince was obsessed with him."

"Was Vince stalking him?" Jeffers asked.

"No, nothing like that. It's more like he wanted to *be* Al. They met at theatre school and ever since it's like Vince has been trying to copy Al in everything. When Al stopped acting and started giving workshops, Vince did the same a few months later. Al took over as artistic director of a children's theatre here in Niagara, and a year later we'd heard that Vince had been hired by a theatre for young audiences in Toronto. When Al finally went into teaching full time, guess who also made the move? I heard he even tried to date men at one point."

"It's possible that's all coincidental."

"Anything's possible but—"

"Were they friends when they were at school together?" I interrupted.

"I don't get the impression they were. Al never said so. There's something off about Vince though. I've felt it every time I've met him. Al was always nice to everyone, but even he got a little unnerved when Vince was around. He'd be polite and professional when they saw one another, but that's all."

"And how often did they see each other?"

"A couple of times a year, I guess. If there was a function for the school board. But that's only recently. Vince didn't work for the Niagara region until a few years ago."

"And now he has Al's job," I mused.

Glynn nodded sadly. "Listen, on the phone you said something about a picture?"

"Um, yeah," I said, handing it over. We didn't really need it now, but as it was what got us this meeting in the first place, I felt I should continue the ruse. "I found it in one of the books in Al's office."

"Look how young he is here. God, he was so beautiful. And that smile. I remember the first time he smiled at me." A small tear ran down Glynn's cheek. "This was in one of Al's books?"

"I assumed it was Al's," I lied. "Come to think of it, it may have been one of Vince's."

"That would make more sense. I can't imagine Al holding on to this. He wasn't a keepsake kind of guy." He handed the photo back to me without commenting on Vince's presence in the picture. "Bella, I know you're going to be working with Vince and I'm sorry if I've coloured your impression of him. Regardless of my feelings, he is, reportedly, a very good teacher. I wonder if you would do a favour for me. For Al actually."

"Sure. If I can."

"Al was coaching a student privately. Secretly, I guess you could say. He told me the girl's family didn't want her taking drama. Her father even came to the school one day and pulled the girl out of class. Since then he's been working with her one-on-one."

"That's pretty risky, going against a parent's wishes," Jeffers said.

"Al tried to work things out. He went to talk to the father but was met with so much resistance. He told me the girl was one of the most promising students he'd ever had. Such raw, natural talent. He knew she was destined for great things and he was excited to have the opportunity to be able to mould and shape and be a part of her development. It was important to Al. She was important to Al. I know he'd want Vince to continue. Will you tell him?"

"Absolutely. Do you know the name of the student?"

"Ellie."

Chapter 8

"Ellie's got to be Elsbeth," I said as soon as we had settled ourselves at a little table in the back of The Old Firehall, one of St. David's two restaurants. "That would explain why she was at the school so early. She wasn't meeting a friend to study. She was meeting Macie for one of their sessions."

"It would also give us a possible motive," Jeffers said. "If her father found out Macie was secretly coaching her, he may have been angry enough—"

"To kill him?" I whispered, finishing Jeffers' thought. "I don't know. It seems a little extreme."

"Samuel, I don't think whoever murdered Macie did so intentionally. The way he died indicates, to me, that he was killed in the heat of the moment. If the father was mad enough, there's no telling what he could have done."

I shook my head. "But Ellie and her family are Mennonite. Violence isn't part of their way of life."

"All the more reason to cover up the murder as a suicide," he said with a wink.

"I'm more interested in Vince Leduc," I said.

"Yeah, that's a possibility too."

"A possibility? You heard Glynn. The man was obsessed with Al Macie."

"'Obsessed' is a bit strong. Just because the guy's career path mirrored Macie's doesn't make him a stalker. They weren't friends. They rarely saw one another. There's nothing to indicate motive. As far as I can tell the two men had very little to do with each other at all." I opened my mouth to object and Jeffers cut me off. "Look, I agree with you there's more to Leduc. There's something ... odd about the whole thing, yes, but I'm just not feeling him for the killer."

"Well, I'm not feeling Ellie's father."

"I should hope not. I think the good doctor would have something to say about that."

"Oh, stop it," I said with a laugh. "You know what I mean."

A waiter came by and we placed our order.

"Listen," Jeffers started when the waiter had gone, "I don't know a lot about Mennonites so I'll take your word for it about the violence thing, but from the little I do know, there's a strong emphasis on family. If Ellie's father felt Macie was a threat to his daughter in any way—"

"A threat? He was giving her acting lessons!"

"Keep your voice down. Maybe there was more to it. We really won't know anything until you talk to the girl."

If Jeffers was right and Macie was killed without intent, I had to admit that an angry father trumped a copycat teacher for the more likely prime suspect. I let out a resigned sigh.

"Now, Samuel, don't pout. If you want to look into Leduc too, go for it. But talk to Ellie first. She's the priority."

"I'm sorry we have to do this like in primary school," Vince said, pulling out the attendance folder. "Once I get to know all of you, this will be much easier; until then, please bear with me." He proceeded to call out names and the students indicated their presence with various "heres," hand waves, and the odd "yo." I did my best to follow along and match faces to the names.

We were in the same studio in which Al Macie had been found. These kinds of theatres are typical for any high school or university training program due to the ability to transform the space easily to meet the needs of any exercise or production. They are also the performance space of choice for experimental theatre or any production that requires an intimate, simple focus. Familiarly known as a black box, it was a large square room with black walls, ceiling, and floor. To go with the black mood that prevailed.

I didn't know how much the students knew of the details of Al's death but rumours fly and kids talk. There was a cloud hanging over the room. A cloud and a grid for lights. Most of the fresnels had been removed during the investigation and were on the floor and off to the side. Looking at the students, I guessed I wasn't the only one who looked at the grid differently.

Black platforms forming five rows each had been arranged on three sides of the square playing space and chairs were stacked at the ends of each row. The class was seated in the centre section. I easily identified Elsbeth Penner among a small group of girls and confirmed she was the girl I had seen crying on the morning of Al Macie's death. As Vince Leduc came to the end of the list of names, I noticed Elsbeth's had not been called.

"Okay," Leduc said, putting the attendance folder in a slot just outside the door, "before we begin, I'd like to officially introduce the amazing Bella James." He stretched out an arm to where I was sitting and the class burst into a round of applause. "Bella is going to be with us a couple of days a week for the next seven weeks, as you know. I mentioned yesterday that most of the focus this week is going to be on getting comfortable with each other. If we are going to be vulnerable together in this room, we have to be able to trust one another. And that goes for Bella too. If you're okay with that?" He talked to the students but directed the last question to me.

"Can't wait." Vince and I had already agreed on what we wanted my role in the class to be, but he wanted to ensure that the students considered me one of the group rather than a special guest.

"I know you all probably have questions for Ms. James and I assure you, there will be plenty of time to pick her brain. But for now, let's all get on our feet and get started."

The students scattered themselves on the floor. Once Elsbeth had found herself a place, I nonchalantly adjusted my own position to be closer to her. We shared a smile and I feigned an apology for not remembering her name.

"Ellie," she said.

"Ah," I said with mock frustration. "I tried to catch all the names during attendance. I must have missed it. I'm sorry."

"Oh, I'm not on the list. Mr. Macie lets me take this class during one of my spares. I mean, he *let* me." Her voice broke off and I saw her sadness behind her eyes. "I haven't talked to Mr. Leduc about it yet."

When I'd arrived earlier I filled Vince in on Al's arrangement with Elsbeth, as per Glynn's request. He promised to help in any way he could. If Ellie came to him.

"I'm sure it won't be a problem," I said, smiling sympathetically.

Vince led us through a physical and vocal warm-up

before launching into a couple of improvisation games and some meatier work. Slowly but surely, the dark clouds that hovered started to clear and the students began to relax into the new normal.

Vince and I had agreed that we would participate in the exercises along with the students for the first week. He was sensitive to the fact that the students were still grieving the loss of their teacher and didn't want to pick up from where Al had left off without establishing some kind of relationship of his own with them. I admired his compassion, in spite of my suspicion that he was somehow involved in Al's murder.

"I think by the end of the week we should be able to get into some of the work Al started with them," Vince said when we were alone after the class had ended. "I know we only have you twice a week but I'd really love for you to take over as much as you want when you're here. There are a number of students auditioning for university programs so it will be especially valuable to them to have your level of expertise to draw from."

"Sounds great, but I'm hardly an expert," I said. "Besides, you were an actor."

He laughed. "A million years ago. And not a very good one at that." He gave me a puzzled look. "How did you know that?"

"The books," I said clumsily, indicating his shelves. I was dangerously close to giving away that I knew much more about him than he thought I did. "They're books actors have. Not teachers. Unless the teachers were once actors," I blathered. "I just assumed."

"Mr. Leduc? I'm sorry to interrupt." Ellie's appearance at the office door brought an end to the subject and saved me from myself. I had to be more careful.

"Not at all," Vince said. "Come on in. Ellie, right?"

"Yes, um…" She looked at me. "Did you tell him?"

I shook my head.

"Have a seat," Vince said. "I'm assuming this is about what you were working on with Mr. Macie?"

"You know about that?"

"Mr. Macie's partner filled me in. He said whatever it is that you two were doing was pretty important to him. If I can help at all, I'd be happy to."

He spoke the words as if he'd really had a conversation with Glynn instead of hearing of Glynn and Al's sentiments through me.

Relief spilled over Ellie. "Mr. Macie let me take this class even though I'm not registered for it. It's a long story but it's really important that there's no record of it on my report card. I'll still do all the assignments and the exams and everything. And I want you to give me a mark; it just can't be official." Vince listened intently. Ellie went on. "I have an audition for The National Theatre School in a couple of weeks. Mr. Macie was helping me with my monologues. It wasn't every day. Just once or twice a week."

"I think I can manage that," Vince said.

"We have to meet during lunch. It has to be lunch. I don't mind if you eat or anything."

"Why lunch?" Vince asked. Ellie hesitated. Vince didn't press her. "It doesn't matter. What pieces are you doing?"

"*The Shape of a Girl* and *As You Like It*."

"Rosalind?"

"Phoebe."

Vince made a face. "Everyone does Phoebe."

"NTS gave us a list to choose from. I really wanted to

do something from *An Inspector Calls*, but they were pretty insistent about Shakespeare for the classical monologue."

"All the schools are. Listen, why don't you come by tomorrow at lunch and we'll see what you've got."

"Really?" she asked. Vince nodded. "Oh, thank you so much." Ellie stood. I don't think I'd ever seen someone so grateful. She moved to the door but turned back quickly. "And I can stay in the class?"

"It wouldn't be the same without you."

She gave an excited squeal. "Thank you, Mr. Leduc. You won't be sorry. I promise." She turned to go.

"Ellie, hang on. I'll walk out with you," I said and grabbed my things. I wanted to get out of the office before Vince remembered what we had been talking about before Ellie arrived.

"*An Inspector Calls*, huh? That's a tough play," I said, as we wormed our way through those students who had not yet made it to their next class.

"The Shaw did it a few years ago. Wallis Canlon played Sheila. I love her. She's amazing. The show was amazing."

"I've heard."

"She's playing Sonia in *Uncle Vanya* this year. I can't wait to see it. Do you know her?"

"Not well but we've met."

I listened to her gush about her idol for a little while longer before I asked if she went to the Festival often.

"Not as much as I'd like. I'd see everything if I could."

I would have loved another couple of hours with Ellie to really gain her trust but a bell rang for the next class. I needed something to bring to Jeffers so I dove in. "Your parents must be pretty proud of you getting an audition for NTS."

"It's just my dad."

"Well, he must be especially thrilled then." Her walking slowed and she fell silent. "Ellie?"

"Ms. James, if I tell you something will you promise not to tell Mr. Leduc?"

"Of course."

"My father doesn't know about NTS."

I stopped. It had been a long time since I'd auditioned for theatre school, but I knew such auditions took place in major city centres. Although NTS likely auditioned across the country I doubted Niagara-on-the-Lake was on its list of stops.

"Ellie, where's the audition?"

"Toronto. If I catch the eight o'clock bus from St. Catharines, I'll have plenty of time to do the audition and be back in Niagara before school's out. My dad will never know."

"Ellie, that's very risky. If something were to happen to you—"

"Nothing will happen! I have it all figured out. It will be fine."

"I'm sure if you explain things to your dad, he'll understand."

"He won't. You don't know, Ms. James. If my dad knew, he'd…"

I could see she was getting upset. "Okay. It's okay," I said. She took a deep breath and seemed to calm. "Do you want to tell me what this has to do with Mr. Leduc?"

"My father found out I was meeting Mr. Macie and, I don't know what he said to him, but Mr. Macie told me he couldn't help me anymore. If Mr. Leduc knew that, he might not—"

"Hold on a sec. Your father went to see Mr. Macie?"

"Yes."

"When was this?"

"The day before…"

"Before he was killed?" Ellie nodded. "Ellie, why were you at the school so early the morning of Mr. Macie's death?"

She looked to the floor and mumbled something about studying for a test.

"Ellie, there was no test, was there?"

Her gaze stayed fixed on the linoleum tiles.

"Ellie—"

"Elsbeth!" We turned to see a boy about fifteen. Like Ellie, he was dressed in the traditional Mennonite style. He was tall and muscular. The kind of muscles one develops from hours of long work outdoors rather than from time spent in a gym. I guessed he was her brother. "Why aren't you in French?"

Ellie's cheeks reddened. "I'm going," she said, then glanced at me. "I just had to show this lady where the library was."

"Yes, thank you," I said, following Ellie's lead. "I'm sure I can find it from here."

"It's at the end of the hall," the boy said, attitude colouring his words.

"Great."

He stared at me, his eyes nearly penetrating the lie. Ellie brushed by me clutching her books to her chest and her head lowered subserviently. The boy caught her arm as she passed him.

"Who is that?"

"I told you, she's nobody. Just some woman looking for the library."

She broke free of his grasp and hurried down the hall. I started walking in the opposite direction. I could feel the boy's eyes on my back. I didn't turn around. There was something about him that sent shivers down my spine.

Chapter 9

"You think she's involved somehow?" Jeffers asked me later that evening.

"I don't know, but I think it's possible. She seems desperate to go through with this audition. Once Macie cut her off, maybe she felt the only way to get the help she needed was to get a new teacher."

Jeffers looked up at me from the floor of my kitchen where he was waiting for Moustache to return the toy lion he had thrown. "Remember, Samuel, that I said Macie was likely killed in the heat of the moment. I know he wasn't a big guy, but I still don't think a seventeen-year-old girl would have the capability—"

"Likely."

"What?"

"You said he was *likely* killed in the heat of the moment. Maybe—"

"Jeez, Bella, maybe nothing. He was. He *was* killed in the heat of the moment. It was a crime of passion. There was no intent. He pissed somebody off and they got angry. Too angry."

Moustache ran into the room with the lion dangling out of his mouth. Jeffers grabbed at it, but the dog held strong and growled playfully. Jeffers won the tug-of-war, threw the lion again, and Moustache flew out of the room in pursuit.

"What if she had help?"

"Bella!"

"I'm just saying what if? Her brother looked strong. Maybe she got him to help her. You know, do the dirty work." Jeffers laughed. "Okay, fine. Maybe she just brought him along to intimidate Macie and things escalated."

Jeffers and Moustache went through their routine again. When the dog dashed out of the room, Jeffers got to his feet and leaned against the counter, his eyes squarely on me.

"That's possible."

"Ha!"

"It's also possible the brother took it upon himself to follow up on whatever threat the father made."

"How do you know there was a threat?"

"Ellie said her father went to see Macie and after that meeting Macie called off their arrangement. Glynn said Macie had tried to reason with the father once before and consciously went against his wishes and continued to work with Ellie. So why stop this time? There had to be some kind of threat."

Moustache ran into the kitchen and was disappointed to find Jeffers standing. Jeffers bent down and ruffled the dog's ears, which seemed to appease him. Moustache wagged his tail then plopped down and proceeded to chew on the lion's head.

"You going to talk to Ellie's father again?"

"You bet. I have to know what that meeting was about."

"Might be a good idea to talk to Glynn again too. He seemed to think Al was still working with Ellie. If Al had been threatened by her father the day before he died, doesn't it seem strange he didn't mention anything to Glynn?"

"You think Glynn's hiding something?" Jeffers asked.

"I don't, actually. I just find it odd Al wouldn't have confided in him."

"So maybe Macie's the one hiding something."

"Or maybe there's a reason he kept the threat to himself. Either way, we should talk to Glynn."

"We?"

"Oh, give me a break. You knew this case would suck me in."

"Of course I did. I'm just surprised it took so long."

"Hello," said a voice from the front hall.

Moustache abandoned the lion and ran out of the room.

"We're in the kitchen," I called.

Paul came in carrying Moustache over his shoulder.

"Hey man," he said to Jeffers.

"Doc."

Paul put the dog down and the two men shook hands.

"You staying for dinner?" Paul asked, coming over to me and planting a kiss on my cheek.

"Not tonight," Jeffers said. "I'm on dinner and diaper duty. Aria informed me she's spending the better part of the evening in a hot bath. Just wanted a quick check in with Bella about our case."

"So it's finally 'our' case is it?" Paul said in an I-told-you-so voice.

"You knew she wouldn't be able to resist forever," Jeffers said.

"I'm just surprised it took this long."

"You, shut up." I directed at Paul, "and you, get out," I said, ushering a laughing Jeffers to the front door.

"Oh hey, did you get anything from Leduc?" Jeffers asked.

"No, there wasn't time. But there was something weird. Before class I told him about how Al had been working with Ellie and how much Glynn said it would mean to Al if Vince would continue. But when Vince relayed the conversation to Ellie he did it as if *he'd* been the one who'd talked to Glynn. Like they were friends and that Glynn had confided in him. There was no acknowledgment whatsoever that Glynn had spoken through me."

"I wouldn't read anything into that. Leduc's the new guy replacing a teacher with whom Ellie obviously had a close relationship. He probably thought she'd feel more comfortable with him if she believed he'd been close with Macie too."

"I don't think that's it. There was something pathological about the way he said it. I could see he truly believed he and Glynn had had that conversation. Look, Glynn said Vince was obsessed with Al. That he wanted to be Al. What if he thinks that in some way he is?

"Like schizophrenic?"

"I don't know. No. I mean, I don't … I'm certainly no expert and I don't believe there's anything medically wrong with Vince, but … You know what, never mind. I'm sure you're right. I'm probably just reading too much into it. Go home to your wife."

"You don't have to tell me twice. What's your day like tomorrow for interviews?"

"I have a costume fitting first thing, then rehearsal all morning. I have a later call in the afternoon, so I have a couple of hours in the middle of the day."

"Perfect. Text me when you're free and I'll pick you up."

"Okay."

Jeffers descended my front steps and then turned back to me. "Bella, if this thing with Leduc is really bothering you, look into it. Don't take my word for it. I'm no expert either. You might just be onto something."

"But you think I'm barking up the wrong tree?"

"Look, the Inspector is itching for results. Just because I think the stronger lead is with Ellie and her family doesn't mean that's the only tree in the forest. Bark away."

I watched Jeffers pull out of the driveway, then closed the door. Paul was standing in the entrance of the kitchen leaning against the wall with his arms crossed.

"What?" I asked.

"I didn't say anything."

"No, but you're thinking it."

"The only thing I'm thinking about is how great you look in those jeans."

"No, you're not, and you know it. You're mad because I told you I wasn't getting involved and now I'm involved."

"I'm not mad, Bells," he said, taking me in his arms. "I'm worried. There's a difference."

"I promise to be careful," I said, pressing my face to his chest. "What's that smell?"

"Oh, sorry," he said, pulling away. "It's pee. A little puppy's first visit and he got very excited. I meant to throw on some scrubs, but the day got away from me."

"You've been walking around all day with puppy pee on you?"

"Occupational hazard," he said, laughing.

"It's disgusting," I said, shaking my head but laughing in spite of myself. "I'm not having dinner with you when you're covered in urine. Go change. Or shower. Or something. But be quick. I'm starving."

Chapter 10

"I'm never eating again!" I said, as I plopped into a chair in the green room opposite Adam and Powell. "You should see my costume for the Mein Herr number."

"Darling, it's *Cabaret*," Adam said. "The whole show is highly sexualized. What did you expect?"

"I knew I'd be showing skin," I said. "I just didn't think I'd be showing quite so much of it."

"You're gorgeous," said Powell. "You have nothing to worry about."

"Says he who spends most of the show in a suit."

"Yes. And that is why I am thoroughly enjoying this bagel," he teased and put the last of his breakfast into his mouth.

At that moment Manda glided into the room with the actor playing Captain Bluntschli in *Arms and the Man*. She laughed at something he said just a little louder than necessary to ensure she had everyone's attention, which she then pretended not to notice.

I groaned as I watched her perfect figure sway this way and that as she placed an order for a coffee. "She's going to look fabulous in that costume."

As if they didn't have enough to do, the costume department had to make duplicates of many costumes for the understudies.

"Stay healthy, my dear, and she'll never get a chance to wear it," Powell said, gathering his things and rising from the table. "If you'll excuse me, I want to brush my teeth before we start. I believe you and I have some kissing on the schedule this morning."

He gave my shoulder a friendly squeeze and left. I noticed he purposely avoided Manda as he passed her and I couldn't help but smile.

"Are you sure he's gay?" I asked Adam.

He rolled his eyes. "Bella, when are you going to accept that this is one field I have way more experience in than you? Now come on, I want to make sure I get my spot in the rehearsal hall."

"You have a 'spot'?" I asked, following him out of the room.

"You betcha. You know how Powell always puts his stuff close to the piano?"

"I haven't noticed."

"He does. And you know that pillar by the stage manager's table?"

I called up a picture of the room in my mind. "The one with the mirror?"

"Yes," Adam said with a wicked grin. "The mirror gives a perfect view of the lovely Mr. Avery and he doesn't even know it. I can stare at him all the livelong day."

It was my turn to roll my eyes. "Why don't you ask him out already?"

"Don't rush me. I'm still working my magic."

"You call that magic, stalking him in a mirror?"

"Oh, stop," he said, pretending to be offended. "So tell me, is he a good kisser?"

"Adam!"

"Come on, James, dish!"

"I will not," I said, laughing. "Ask him out. Go on a date and find out for yourself."

"But you could save me the time and effort."

"Nope," I said. "Maybe you should ask the director to build in a kiss between Cliff and Ernst," I said, referring to the characters Powell and Adam played.

"That's not a bad idea," he said, the wheels clearly turning at Mach speed. "It would be weird at the time to have a gay Nazi, but there are certainly undertones to Cliff..."

"You probably see gay undertones in a weather report."

"Sweetheart, don't even get me started."

"Does it ever bother Paul? You kissing other people on stage?" Jeffers asked, as we drove to Ellie Penner's home.

"Should it?"

"I don't think Aria would like it if I spent my days kissing other women."

"I'm sure she wouldn't given your line of work, but in my business, it's just another day at the office. I spend my days pretending to be other people. And sometimes those pretend people have to kiss other pretend people. But the kissing isn't real. It's like if my character has to shoot someone. I don't *really* shoot them. "

Jeffers shook his head. "It's different. Your lips are touching."

"Yeah, but..." I fumbled over how exactly to explain in a way Jeffers would understand. "There's no tongue."

Jeffers looked at me sideways. "I have been to movies, Bella. I have seen that kind of kissing and I can tell you that there, most definitely, *is* tongue."

"First of all, this isn't a movie. That's a whole other ... and secondly, you're in a room full of people. There's no intimacy. There's a detachment. Everything is talked through beforehand. It's basically choreographed."

"Choreographed?"

"Not like a dance—well, sometimes—but more like working out the mechanics of it."

"'Mechanics.' How romantic."

"See?"

Jeffers shrugged. "It's still weird."

Thankfully we pulled in to a long driveway and the matter was dropped.

Ellie's house was a white-brick, ranch-style bungalow with green shutters and matching window boxes. It was set far back from the road, which allowed for a very large front yard that was neatly kept but sparsely landscaped. It reminded me of the lawns back on PEI, sprawling and green but without much shrubbery or floral enhancements. The nearest neighbour's house was a little further down the road on the opposite side. The driveway ended at a grey garage door and Jeffers and I got out.

When our knocking went unanswered, we made our way around to the back of the house where a large patio area looked out over acres of orchard. There was a large barn with its doors open. Jeffers and I started along the pebbled path that led toward them when a young man in his twenties emerged pushing a wheelbarrow.

"Excuse me," Jeffers called, holding out his badge.

The man set his load down. In spite of the spring briskness, he pulled a handkerchief from his back pocket, removed his straw hat, and wiped sweat from his forehead. His long pants were held up by suspenders, and the sleeves of his button-down shirt had been rolled up, revealing muscular forearms. I saw Ellie in his face and took him to be yet another brother.

"Detective," the young man said, holding out his hand to shake Jeffers'. "Nice to see you again." His tone was friendly. A far cry from what his brother's had been at the school. "Everything all right?"

"Fine. Corney, right?" Jeffers asked.

"Yes, sir," Corney said, beaming at having been remembered.

"Corney, we need another word with your father. Is he around?"

The young man gestured to where a cart was parked amongst the trees. "It was a hard winter," he said. "Our cherry trees made it through with no injury, but some of our peach trees weren't so lucky."

"I'm sorry to hear that," Jeffers said.

"Oh, they'll be fine," Corney said. "Da's got the magic touch. This about Ellie's teacher again?"

"We just have a few follow-up questions."

"So you haven't caught the guy." It was not a question. "You want me to fetch him?" he asked, indicating his father.

"No, that's all right. I see you're busy."

Jeffers and I said our thanks and moved off in the direction of the cart. Corney picked up his wheelbarrow and watched us go. It wasn't until we were well within the trees that he moved along in the opposite direction.

"Corney?" I asked, as we made our way through the orchard.

Jeffers shrugged. "Probably short for Cornelius."

"Named after his father?"

"No. His father is Armin. Could be a nickname."

"I can think of better nicknames."

"I can think of worse," Jeffers said with a mischievous twinkle in his eye.

We arrived at the cart, and a man dressed almost identical to Corney looked out from behind one of the trees. His expression darkened when he saw Jeffers. "Detective."

"Mr. Penner. I hope this isn't a bad time."

"I'm assuming this visit has something to do with Al Macie."

"Just a few more questions if you wouldn't mind."

Ellie's father set a pair of pruning shears against the trunk of the tree and took off his work gloves. Like Corney, he pulled a handkerchief from his pocket and dabbed at his forehead.

"Not sure what more I can tell you," he said, as he joined us by the cart. He had a long greying beard and piercing blue eyes, which he fixed on me.

"This is my partner, Ms. James," Jeffers said in introduction.

"Pleasure, ma'am," Mr. Penner said, tipping his straw hat to me, but indicating none of the pleasure he spoke of. He reached into the cart and pulled out a thermos. "I'm sorry I don't have anything to offer you," he said, taking a swig from the container. "I wasn't expecting company."

"We're fine," I said.

"Mr. Penner, we'd like to talk to you about a meeting you had with Al Macie," Jeffers said.

"As I told you before, Detective, I was surprised to learn that my daughter was taking drama. Her focus should be on practical courses and I felt Mr. Macie's class would distract her from more important studies." I bristled when he said "more important" but held my tongue. He continued. "I don't expect you to understand, but our way of life is different and the kinds of things that are taught in such a class are not in keeping with the path we follow.

Elsbeth told me she would drop the class. I thought the matter done. However, when I found she'd been deceitful, I went to the school myself and had her removed."

Jeffers opened his mouth to speak but I beat him to it. "How did you find out Ellie was taking the class in the first place?"

"My youngest, Leland, told me about a presentation Elsbeth had been a part of."

I flashed back to Ellie's brother at the school and recalled how he had managed her and seemed to know every detail of her schedule. "Did Leland tell you that Ellie had not dropped the class like she'd promised?"

"I'm not sure what you're implying, Ms. James."

"She's not implying anything," Jeffers said. "Mr. Penner, I was actually referring to a meeting you had with Mr. Macie following Ellie's removal from the class. From what I understand—"

Armin Penner raised a hand to silence Jeffers. "Again, as I've already told you, Mr. Macie showed up here, praising Elsbeth's talent and potential and asking me to reconsider. I told you the same as I told him: such a class is quite simply not in Elsbeth's best interests. She has responsibilities here. To her family. I don't mean to be rude, but we've been through all of this and I really do need to take advantage of what time I have with the sun."

"Mr. Penner, if you'd let me finish, you would know the meeting I wish to speak to you about is the one that took place the day before Mr. Macie died."

Armin Penner hardened a stare on Jeffers. He raised the thermos to his lips one more time, closed the cap, and tossed it back into the cart.

"Is it true you went to see Al Macie at the school shortly before he was found dead?" Jeffers asked.

"It is."

"Mr. Penner, I need you to tell me everything about that meeting."

Armin spoke slowly. "I had learned my daughter was seeing Mr. Macie privately. Some kind of coaching."

"And how did you learn that?" Jeffers asked.

Armin took a deep breath before answering. When he spoke, his voice was firm and his jaw tight. "My son had come upon them that morning and he informed me when he came home for lunch. I immediately went to the school. Mr. Macie was in his office. He knew at once why I had come. He tried again to appeal on Elsbeth's behalf. I told him his relationship with my daughter was not appropriate and that their meetings were to cease immediately; otherwise I would have no choice but to speak with Principal Harvey."

"Not appropriate?" I asked.

"Ms. James, with the exception of myself, her brothers, and certain family relations, Elsbeth is not to be alone in the company of any man. Not until she is married."

"But Al Macie was her teacher. He wasn't just any man."

"I made myself very clear on a number of occasions that his was a class my daughter was not to have any involvement with. Therefore, he was not her teacher and the fact that she persisted on seeing him although I had expressly forbidden it is an even greater indication of her sin."

I'd not had much of a religious upbringing, although my grandmother had taken me to church when I first went to live with her. During one sermon the minister read a passage from the Bible that said, "The soul who sins shall die," and I started wailing, believing my parents' accident to have been punishment for them having been bad people. I loved my parents and couldn't imagine anything they'd done had been bad enough to warrant such a sentence.

They hadn't sinned. God had been wrong. I refused to go to church again after that. Of course, I knew now that that's not how things work, but hearing Armin Penner talk about his daughter's "sin" made me wonder if *he* knew it.

"How did the meeting resolve?" Jeffers asked.

"Mr. Macie apologized and assured me he would bring an end to their arrangement immediately. I thanked him and left."

"And did he?"

"Elsbeth didn't say as much, as that would mean confessing her transgression, but that night I heard her crying in her room and concluded that Mr. Macie had been true to his word." He took a moment to consider his next words. "My daughter ... is ... has always been ... somewhat of a dreamer. She's very much like her mother in that way. When she was growing up, it was really quite delightful. But she is almost eighteen now. And with her mother gone, she has responsibilities. There are rules. She knows that."

"Did you have any other contact with Al Macie that we should know about?"

"I did not. I learned of his death when the school called and asked me to come tend to Elsbeth. I was saddened to hear of it. He struck me as a good man. I'm sure he meant no harm. My daughter can be ... very clever about getting what she wants."

"Do you know why she was at the school so early that morning?"

"She told me she was meeting a girlfriend to study for a test."

"Where was Leland that morning?" I asked.

"Leland? The boys are usually up and at their chores come sunrise. The farm keeps us all busy. They know what they have to do. I don't supervise." The blue of his eyes iced over as he looked at me.

"Thank you, Mr. Penner," Jeffers interjected. "I think that's all for now. We'll let you get back."

"Ms. James," Armin said, as we moved to leave, "it is contrary to our faith to take the life of one that God has created."

I smiled. "I wish everyone believed that."

We passed the barn on our way back to the car in time to meet Corney coming out nursing a bleeding nose and Leland not far behind.

"Dammit, Lee," Corney said, spitting a few drops of blood onto the ground.

"You watch your mouth. And I better not see anything like this again," Leland said, indicating the iPod in his hand before stomping off in the direction of his father. The headphones still hung from Corney's ears. I checked the time. Lunch.

"This is why Ellie was so insistent that her meetings with Vince happen at lunch," I whispered to Jeffers. "Leland comes home. I bet it's the only time he's not monitoring her."

"Because he's monitoring *him*," Jeffers said, nodding to Corney, who looked at us, smiled weakly, then retreated to the barn. "The faith might frown on taking a life, but obviously punching one's brother in the face gets a pass."

"Or maybe Leland thinks some rules don't apply to him."

"Some? Or all?"

Chapter 11

I convinced Jeffers to stop by the school before heading up to see Glynn. Something Armin Penner had said wasn't sitting well with me and, if my hunch was correct, it was for good reason.

I left Jeffers in the car and climbed the steps to the school two at a time. Gerald Harvey was coming out of his office as I made my entrance.

"Just the person I was hoping to see," I said, catching the principal off guard.

"Bella. Ms. James. This isn't one of your days, is it?"

"No. I was hoping to have a word with you."

"I'm on my way to a meeting. You're welcome to walk with me."

"This shouldn't take long," I said, falling into stride.

Harvey cleared his throat and used his forefinger to loosen the collar of his shirt, which was all but swallowed up by his set of chins.

"Mr. Harvey, if a parent were to come to you believing a teacher was having an inappropriate relationship with their child—" Gerald Harvey's pace slowed. "I'm not saying anything has happened," I added quickly, "I'm simply curious as to what steps would be taken to investigate?"

He stopped and turned to look me square in the face. "Ms. James, believe me when I say that words of that nature are things no principal ever wants to hear." He exhaled deeply and resumed walking. "The word 'inappropriate' suggests … sexual misconduct."

"But surely not all claims are sexual? Isn't it possible that—"

"Anything's possible, Ms. James, but the implication, whether true or not, is that some kind of sexual behaviour has taken place."

"And what happens when a claim like that is made? That a teacher has been 'inappropriate'?"

"All complaints are subject to a lengthy inquiry. I'm sure it's no different from any other investigation. Everything is done fairly and impartially, but," he shook his head, "usually the damage has been done. While there has been truth behind many an accusation, and those teachers punished severely, there have also been many innocent teachers whose reputations and careers have been ruined." He stopped again. "I'm sorry, Ms. James, I have to ask, is there something I should know?"

"No. Thank you. This has been very helpful."

"We take complaints of this nature very seriously, whether they are made by parents … or colleagues?"

"Everything's fine. I promise. I just wanted some clarification. I'm sorry to keep you."

I left Harvey looking after me and ran out of the school to where Jeffers was waiting.

"You were right," I said, getting into the car.

"Usually am," he said with a wink.

"Remember you said Armin Penner must have threatened Al Macie in some way in order to get him to stop seeing Ellie once and for all?"

"Yes. But after talking with Penner today, I'm not sure there was any indication of that."

"Oh, but there was. Mr. Penner accused Macie of having an inappropriate relationship with Ellie. Remember?"

Jeffers nodded. "And that he would go to the principal if he didn't stop coaching her."

"Right. According to Gerald Harvey, in situations like these, the word 'inappropriate' immediately implies 'sexual.' If Macie didn't end things with Ellie and *if* Penner had been true to his word and had gone to Gerald Harvey with his complaint, Macie's career would have been over. His reputation would have been ruined. He'd have lost everything."

"Nice catch, Samuel. All right, we know Macie would have understood the seriousness of the insinuation. The question is, did Penner?"

"He knew perfectly well," Glynn said furiously, pacing the length of his living room. "You said Armin Penner, right?" Jeffers and I nodded. "Armin Penner ran for Lord Mayor here several years ago. Lost by a landslide but not for lack of political savvy, I'll give him that. Trust me, he knows the kind of implications a word like 'inappropriate' has. I don't believe this. Al would never have…" Glynn's anger started to give way to grief. "It's no wonder Al gave in. Teaching was everything to him. Amazing, isn't it? How much power one little word has?"

Jeffers and I exchanged a look. "Glynn, are you sure we're talking about the same Armin Penner?" I asked. "Penner's family is Old Order Mennonite. From the little I know of the faith, any kind of political participation is often rejected. Even voting."

"Well, the Armin Penner I know wasn't any Old Order Mennonite. But how many Armin Penners are there around here? It's got to be the same man," Glynn said, as he slumped into an armchair and crossed his legs. One of the Great Danes got up from where it was sleeping in the corner of the room and dropped its gigantic head in Glynn's lap. He stroked it lovingly.

"How long ago was this?" Jeffers asked.

"Four, maybe five years ago."

Jeffers scribbled in his notebook while I mentally filed away the fact there was obviously more to Armin Penner than we realized.

"Mr. Radley, I take it from your reaction that Al never mentioned this?" Jeffers said. Glynn shook his head. "Do you have any idea why he would keep something like this from you?"

"He wouldn't." He raised the dog's head up to his own and gave it a gentle kiss on the forehead. As if it were some kind of signal, the dog trotted into the kitchen. Glynn then got up from the chair slowly. A man weighed down by grief and the promise of emptiness around every turn. "I have to feed the dogs. Can I get you anything? I'm going to make some tea."

"Tea would be nice," I said.

There was a partial view into the kitchen from where I sat in the living room. Just enough so one could still entertain guests while cooking but not have the full mess on display. From what I was able to see, the kitchen didn't look as if it had had much use of late. I guessed the dogs were the only ones eating. And perhaps only Roger at that, as Edith had not been seen since we'd arrived.

"I have a bit of a temper," Glynn said from the kitchen. "We do twenty-four hour shifts and need to be focused so Al would often wait to tell me things he knew would set me off until I got home. Didn't want me distracted in case we got a call. I've only got Earl Grey."

"That's fine," I said.

"Every time I left for work, Al would say, 'Come home to me.' Because I was the one with the dangerous job. Or so we thought." Glynn came into the living room with a small dish of something orange. "Edith hasn't been able to keep her food down. The only thing she seems to be able to tolerate is puréed yams." He looked at the dish sadly and disappeared down the hall.

Jeffers and I waited until we were sure Glynn was out of earshot before turning to each other.

"Is it the same Armin Penner?" I whispered.

"I don't know," Jeffers said.

"How can you not know? You're from here. Don't you follow local politics? How do you vote?"

"This isn't my riding, Samuel."

"But he would have been in the news."

Jeffers shrugged.

"If Armin Penner the politician and Armin Penner the overbearing father are indeed one and the same, that means the conversion to Old Order Mennonite practices is relatively recent," I said. "It would certainly explain why Corney was sneaking time with his iPod and why Ellie's dreams extend well beyond her faith."

"And why Leland still thinks with his fists."

"Of the three children, Leland strikes me as the one who has embraced it most of all."

"That may well be, Samuel, but some things are just inherent and it's obvious that kid has one hell of a mean streak."

"Did he kill Al?" Glynn asked from the hallway.

The question caught me by surprise and I quickly looked to Jeffers.

"We don't know, Glynn, I'm sorry," Jeffers said. "I'm afraid our leads are few, but I assure you we are following all of them."

"But it's possible. Right?" Glynn persisted. Jeffers remained silent. "Oh, come on. You just said the old man threatened Al. So it is conceivable that his son took it upon himself to—"

"Glynn," Jeffers said, raising his voice slightly, "At this time, it is not something we're considering. However—"

"Why not?" Glynn was on the verge of becoming hysterical and I couldn't help but agree with him. Somebody killed Al. Why not Leland Penner?

"The boy is fifteen years old," Jeffers explained, calmly, "I'm sure you can imagine what kind of damage an accusation like that would do to a young man." Jeffers likened an accusation against Leland's to the one Armin Penner had levied on Al. He was right, of course. The last thing we needed was for the grieving widower to take it upon himself to seek vengeance. Especially when there was nothing to go on other than the fact that the kid was creepy and a bully to his siblings. Eventually Glynn's shoulders slumped, his eyes closed, and his body sought the support of the wall. "Glynn, I promise you, we are doing everything we can to find Al's killer."

Glynn nodded. The kettle started to whistle. Glynn looked to be in no state to deal with it so I excused myself to fix the tea. When I returned moments later, neither Jeffers nor Glynn had moved.

"Glynn," Jeffers said, still using the calm voice, "there is something else we'd like to ask you about."

Jeffers looked to me. I looked back, skeptical. "What?" I mouthed.

I lip-read Jeffers' response, "Leduc."

"No," I said, voiceless.

"Just do it," was Jeffers' soundless reply.

A sigh from Glynn brought an end to our silent exchange. Jeffers raised an eyebrow in my direction.

"Glynn," I started reluctantly, "I'd like to talk to you a bit more about Vince."

Glynn groaned. Peeled himself off the wall and resumed his seat in the armchair. "What's the guy done now? I suppose he's been given Al's promotion?"

"Al's promotion?"

"It hadn't been announced yet, but Al was taking over as the new drama consultant for the district. It was going to take him out of the classroom, which he wasn't thrilled about, but he was even less thrilled about what the government cuts were doing to the curriculum. Especially where drama was concerned. He felt that, as consultant, he'd really be able to make a difference. Change people's way of thinking, you know? Show them why it's so important the arts be given equal attention. Equal value." Glynn smiled at the memory. "You couldn't have a better advocate for the arts in the schools than Al. Certainly not Vincent Leduc."

"Why do you think he'd be offered the job?"

"He got Al's class. I just assumed."

"And why would Vince be such a bad choice?"

"Because Vincent Leduc only cares about Vincent Leduc," Glynn shifted in his seat as his words took on more vehemence. "Actually, no, that's not true. The only thing Vince cares about or, I suppose I should say, *cared* about, was Al."

"You mentioned before that Vince was always competing with Al. That he had a kind of obsession with him."

"To put it mildly," Glynn scoffed.

Jeffers and I exchanged a look.

"Is there anything more you can tell us about that?" Jeffers put in. "Other than Vince's career seeming to mirror Al's—"

"It *did*! It didn't 'seem' to, it did."

"All right. I'm sorry." Jeffers took a breath. "Was there ever anything else in Vince's behaviour? Did he ever threaten Al? Or you?" Glynn shook his head. "Did he ever do anything that might support your claim that Vince's interest in Al went beyond—"

"Have you met him, Detective?"

"No."

"But Bella has." Glynn turned appealing eyes to me. "You can't quite put your finger on it. But there's something about him that's ... not right. You must have felt it."

I nodded ever so slightly, which seemed to appease.

"To answer your question, Detective, no, Vince has never threatened us. But just because he's never done anything untoward or been troublesome in any way doesn't make me wrong."

Jeffers looked pensive. His brow was furrowed and his eyes moved haphazardly around the room. I'd seen this kind of thing before. Jeffers' mind was racing. "Do you think he could have killed Al?" he asked.

Glynn let out a guttural laugh. "No way. That would be like killing a part of himself."

"Maybe the part that's been standing in his way," Jeffers said.

***

"Think about it. If Vince has been following in Al's footsteps all this time, wouldn't he want to get ahead eventually?" Jeffers asked when we'd returned to the car. We'd left poor Glynn to ponder the possibilities that not one but two people may have wanted the love of his life dead. "Maybe the only way he felt he could do that was to eliminate the competition."

"But Jeffers, we don't know if there really was any competition."

"Glynn said—"

"I know what Glynn said, but there's nothing to support it. You said yourself this was a weak lead."

"I'm not so sure now. I want to meet him. I need to see for myself what you and Glynn both think is so off about the man. That'll give me a better idea how to proceed. Or if. Maybe it will just put me right back to square one."

"The Penners?"

Jeffers nodded. "I'm going to head back to the station and see what more I can learn about Armin Penner and his family. You want me to drop you at home or at the theatre?"

"Home. I've still got some time before rehearsal. I think I'll do a little digging myself."

"Great. I'll check in with you later. We can compare notes. And when are you at the school again?"

"Tomorrow."

"I'm going to try to pop in. See what I can get off Leduc. Macie's death has to be tied to him or one of the Penners. If I can look at them side by side, maybe it'll be clearer as to which."

Chapter 12

Glynn Radley had been generous when he'd said Armin
Penner had lost his bid for Lord Mayor by a landslide. He
had taken a walloping from what I gleaned from my
Internet search. I skimmed over the articles that detailed his
platform and political history and stopped when I got to
one that showed a picture of all the candidates and their
wives at some sort of luncheon. I switched my search to
Images and a larger version of the picture filled my screen.
Armin Penner was joined by his wife, Adele. Both wore
stylish outfits and beaming smiles. They appeared to be
engaged in easy conversation with the others at their table.
A further search uncovered another photograph in which
Armin, Adele, and the three younger Penners posed in
front of a campaign sign on the front lawn of their home.

Adele was beautiful. Rich, chestnut-coloured hair fell to
her shoulders in a gentle wave that kissed her high
cheekbones along the way. Her eyes were big and bright,
and her smile exploded off the page. Armin had a sparkle
in his eyes there'd been no evidence of when we'd met.
The two boys were dressed tastefully in chinos and
collared shirts, their arms draped around one another's
shoulders in brotherly solidarity. Ellie, the spitting image
of her mother, wore a floral print dress and an expression
that indicated, even then, her flair for the dramatic. They

looked like the perfect political family trying to convince the masses that a vote for Penner was a vote well cast. And they looked happy. The picture may have been posed, but the sentiment therein was real.

I typed Adele's name into the search engine but came up empty. There was nothing to indicate whether she had died, left, or been abducted by aliens. Nothing about the Penners at all following the election. I fired off a text to Jeffers with Adele's name and received a quick response that he was one step ahead of me. I waited for more but my phone remained silent.

I looked at the two pictures again and wondered how the happy people smiling back at me could have undergone such a transformation. What had led to the loss of Armin's sparkle and the rift between the brothers? What had awakened Leland's darker nature? Why did Ellie feel the need to shroud her dreams in secrecy and deceit? Adele held the answers, I was sure of that. Or rather, whatever happened to her. And I hoped Jeffers was having more luck in discovering just what, exactly, that was.

"She died," Powell Avery whispered in the middle of rehearsal. We were supposed to be frozen on one part of the stage while a scene took place on another, but the actors involved in the other scene kept getting stuck on a particularly complicated bit of business so Powell and I had dropped the convention and were engaged in quiet conversation.

"Adele Penner?"

"Hospital botch up."

"What does that mean?"

"You know, someone goes in for something routine and … things don't go quite as planned. It was a pretty big story here for a while. Big lawsuit filed by the family and whatnot and then it all just disappeared."

"Are you sure? I couldn't find anything like that when I looked online."

"No, you wouldn't. The husband was a local politician. Kept it out of the papers. And saw to it that everything was buried after the settlement went through."

"Then how do you know all this?"

"The guy I was dating at the time. His sister was one of the doctors named in the lawsuit. The whole thing was awful. In the end, the hospital was cleared of any wrongdoing and the death was ruled a tragic accident."

"But there was still a settlement?"

"A 'gesture of sympathy and condolence.'"

I rolled my eyes and chuckled at his turn of phrase. The stage manager gave us a look and put a finger up to her lips as a warning to be quiet. Powell and I both nodded our apologies.

"Do you remember what procedure Adele went in for? What went wrong?"

He shook his head. "This was years ago. Why do you want to know all this?"

"Just curious." I deflected. "Her daughter is in the class I'm working with. I've heard some rumblings, that's all."

He opened his mouth to say something further but an arched eyebrow from the stage manager brought an end to our exchange.

We sat for another five minutes like reprimanded schoolchildren before the director announced we'd be going back and picking up from the middle of our scene. Powell and I got into position, delivered our lines, and held the freeze while the scene that followed played out smoothly, devoid of all earlier complications. When we finished, Powell was hauled off in one direction by the music director and I, in another, by the choreographer, which left the conclusion of poor Adele Penner's story untold and lingering amidst the opening chords of "It Couldn't Please Me More."

"A pineapple? For me?" I joked, as Paul handed off a bag of groceries, the crown of the fruit peeking out of the top. Moustache ran to sniff the legs of Paul's pants, which were covered in invisible details of his day. When finally able, Paul joined me in the kitchen and the dog retreated to his chair in the living room to enjoy his olfactory high.

"Well, this is a nice surprise," he said, wrapping his arms around my waist and drawing me close. "I expected to find you and Jeffers hunched over top-secret files or whatever it is you do."

"Well, we don't hunch, for one thing. And Jeffers is—"

"Sorry, I'm late," Jeffers said, letting himself in.

Paul's arms loosened and his head fell back in resignation. With an understanding smile, he planted a kiss on my forehead and moved to pour himself a glass of wine.

"So," Jeffers said upon entering the kitchen, Moustache at his heels, "what have we got?"

"Adele Penner died," I said.

"I meant for dinner, but okay, let's jump right in."

"Some sort of hospital error."

"Close, Samuel. There was no error," Jeffers corrected. "She went in to have a kidney stone removed and had an allergic reaction to the meds. Died on the table." He deposited Adele's hospital records on the island. "It happens. It's tragic, but it happens."

"But there was a payout," I said. "The Penner family filed a lawsuit and received a settlement."

"Who told you this?"

"I have sources too."

"Huh. Interesting. I didn't find anything about any payment, so if there was one it was done on the downlow." He took the glass of red Paul held out to him and lost himself in contemplation for a moment. "Well done, Samuel," he said finally, clinking his glass against mine. "We'll make a detective of you yet."

I saw Paul's shoulders tense. He caught me looking and covered by giving me a wink and refilling my glass.

"So it's clear the Penners converted to Old Order after Adele's death. We don't know for certain if that was the cause, but it certainly seems likely." I said.

"You thinking it was some kind of rejection of modern medicine?" Jeffers asked.

Paul shook his head. "Mennonites value the healthcare system just like the rest of us. It was likely grief. If they were active in the church before her death, it makes sense they would seek deeper comfort in the faith. People tend to retreat when they're grieving. Withdraw. I bet it's more likely that than any kind of rebuff."

While Paul and Jeffers continued the conversation, I fiddled with fixing dinner. I knew all too well about retreating in times of grief. Usually only people who have done so themselves can recognize it in others. Paul and I had talked about my parents' death and my journey through the grieving process, but he had never shared an experience of his own. Listening to him now made me wonder if grief was something he was better acquainted with than I thought.

"You seemed to be speaking from experience," I said to him later that night. I was lying with my head on his chest. His arms were wrapped around me and the bed covers were wrapped around us.

"More than I'd like," he said. "The death of a pet is as real a loss as any other. I feel it differently from the owners, of course, but I feel it. Each and every time."

"You think it will be hard when Brimstone goes?"

He laughed. "I know you hate that cat, but he's…" His voice trailed off and I felt his chest constrict under my hand.

"You okay?"

"Fine." He stroked my shoulder gently but didn't say anything more.

"I don't hate the cat," I said, breaking the silence. He smiled and squeezed me close.

"He's a hard one to love, I'll give you that. But I do. And, yes, it will be hard when he goes."

He shifted his position and pulled me against him. I was sure Paul's experience with grief extended beyond his patients but I wasn't about to push it. If he wanted to share, he would.

I thought back on myself and the years it took before I was willing, let alone able, to talk about my parents. I snuggled against him, relishing the strength of his embrace, his warm breath on my neck, and how my hair caught on the day's growth on his chin. I was happy. And I was grateful. There was a time when I thought something like this, like him, would never have been a part of my story. I thought about Glynn Radley and Armin Penner sleeping with the ghosts of loves lost and how quickly their own stories had changed. And I thought of Vincent Leduc, who had spent his life chasing the shadow of a man he could never have. Or be. I wondered what that would do to a man. How long could he carry on, surviving on photographs, fuelled by someone else's success? How long before something like that took its toll?

Chapter 13

I was glad to see that Vince had not yet arrived when I got to the school the following morning. I'd been carrying the stolen photograph with me for what seemed like ages and was anxious to be rid of it. I'd just managed to slip it under his desk when he came in.

"You're here early," he said.

"I hope you don't mind."

"Not at all. You can help me get the room set up. Before continuing with the scenes, I want to do some work on independent activities. These kids are so busy 'acting' that if we can get them to stop watching themselves while they're performing, it might be helpful."

"Sounds good. You're doing the person A, person B exercise?" I asked, referring to an exercise whereby person A takes up an independent activity that is hard to do. They must have a life-altering reason for doing what they're doing and a serious consequence if they fail. Person B comes into the scene having prepared a completely different personal circumstance, such as achieving a lifelong dream, or the death of someone close. A's focus is on the task and B's focus is on A. Both people have different emotional lives and are focusing on something other than themselves, which usually forces the pair to act naturally rather than "theatrically." The exercise was one of Sanford Meisner's and had been adopted by many training programs to emphasize the reality of doing.

"I've asked them to come in prepared to be A *and* B. Fingers crossed," Vince said, taking a number of papers from his briefcase and depositing them onto his desk. He'd given me the perfect cue.

"Oops, you dropped this," I said, picking up the photograph from the floor and taking a moment to look at it. "Is this you?"

"Where did you find that?"

"On the floor. You probably dropped it just now when you were emptying your case."

I held out the photo to him. He looked at it but didn't take it. He gave an almost imperceptible glance toward the bookshelf. I immediately thought of one of those stalkers from the movies who keeps trophies of his obsessions, each one in its very specific place.

"Oh my goodness," I said, carefully carrying on the charade, "is this Al Macie?"

"We were at theatre school together," Vince said, taking the picture from me. "Look at us, eh. We both still had hair." He laughed and put the photo into a drawer.

"I didn't realize you two had such a history."

"Theatre school's a funny place. I don't know about your class, but mine was together every day, all day, for three years. By graduation, we'd seen each other in all of our raw and vulnerable glory. We all felt like we'd survived something. Kind of binds you for life, you know?"

I was positive no one from my university days would feel about me the way Vince had just described, but I nodded in solidarity.

Jeffers stuck his head in the office and I waved him in. "Vince, this is—"

"Andre," Jeffers said extending his hand.

I knew from past experience that when Jeffers withheld his last name and title, he was hoping to pass as one of us common folk. I thought his doing so here was an odd choice as he'd already interviewed many of the students and staff in his official capacity. And he was definitely on a first-name basis with Principal Harvey. Just about anyone at the school could knock on Vince's office door and his cover would be blown. I didn't know what he was playing at.

"I hope I'm not interrupting," Jeffers said.

"Not at all," Vince said. "We're just going over our plan for the morning. Are you from the Shaw?"

"Oh no, I'm not theatrical," Jeffers said. "Although, my grandmother said my Deadeye Dick was the best thing in my grade-five production of *H.M.S. Pinafore*."

"Dick Deadeye," Vince said.

"I'm sorry?"

"It's Dick Deadeye."

"What did I say?"

"Deadeye Dick."

"Hmm."

"It's not a big deal," Vince said. "It's just … it's …"

"No! Thank you," Jeffers said in earnest. "All these years I've been bragging erroneously, it seems." There was a long pause during which we all chuckled and smiled politely. "Anyway, I just wanted to give this to Bella and then I will be on my way."

Jeffers gave me a brown paper bag and one of those smiles where the eyebrows raise so high you think they're going to recede into the hairline.

"Some leftovers," Jeffers explained. "Bella's nuts for my wife's cooking."

Vince looked at me. I shrugged and nodded in agreement. The whole situation was so incredibly awkward, I wanted to climb into the lunch bag and die amongst its contents.

"Okay then," Jeffers said with a clap of his hands, "my work here is done."

He and Vince said their goodbyes and I saw him to the door.

"What the hell was that?" I whispered.

"Meet me outside in five minutes?"

"I have a class starting."

"It'll be quick. They haven't even done the anthem yet. You'll be back in time."

I nodded and went back into the office. A few seconds later my phone vibrated, notifying me of a text message. It was from Jeffers: *The guy's a psychopath!*

"He's an egocentric. Highly self-assured. Did you see how he corrected me? He couldn't help himself," Jeffers explained when I met him in the parking lot.

"You did that on purpose?"

"Clever, huh? You'd never guess it was a test."

"Jeffers, just because he corrected you doesn't make him a psychopath."

"He's charming. They almost always are. But it's superficial, you know. All part of the manipulation. The need to be in control."

"Jeffers—"

"You said you've witnessed him lying and that there was something compulsive about it."

"Yes, but—"

"And the fact that he's leeched on to Al Macie for all these years. It's what psychopaths do. Part of their nature. They cling to others to fulfill their own needs."

"There's been no clinging—"

"They spend years planning their revenge. That's why they're so hard to catch. Because every detail of their plan is designed to ensure they get away with it. In Vince's case, he has been fuelled by something that happened with Macie years ago. If what Glynn has told us is true, and I believe it to be—"

"Since when? You haven't seen Vince as a viable suspect. He's been nothing more than a pet project of mine."

"That's true. But now that I've met the man, I can see things more clearly."

"And what you see is a psychopath?"

"Maybe not full blown, but there are definite tendencies."

"You barely spent ten minutes with the guy! And half that time was spent debating the cast list of a Gilbert and Sullivan operetta!"

"Bella, it is my job to recognize people like this."

"You are a homicide detective, Jeffers. Not a psychologist. I don't care how much training you've had or how good you think you are, you are not qualified to decide if someone is a psychopath, a sociopath, or a telepath in as little time as you spent with Vince."

Jeffers crossed his arms and leaned back against his car. For a few moments neither of us spoke.

"You know, a lot of psychopaths have jobs and relationships," Jeffers said, petulantly.

I looked at Jeffers and shook my head. He exhaled loudly and ran his hands through his hair.

"You want to tell me what this is all about?" I asked. "This isn't like you."

He let his arms fall to his sides, resignedly. "I'm getting heat from Morris. He wants to see movement on this case and all I seem to be able to give him are half-baked theories."

"Well, psychopaths aside, I do think you've touched on something as far as Vince is concerned." Jeffers raised his eyebrows. "I think you're right about something happening between him and Al years ago. My guess is it was when they were at school together."

"You think you can find out?"

I shrugged. "He keeps his cards pretty close to his chest."

"That's another sign of—"

"Shut up."

Jeffers nodded and turned to go.

"Did you really play Dick Deadeye? I thought you'd never been to the theatre until last season?"

"I was in grade five and was so terrified, I threw up on my shoes right before I had to go on. The pillow that was supposed to be my hunchback kept sliding down and I could never remember which leg had the limp."

I guffawed.

"Laugh as you will, my grandmother maintained to the day she died that it was the finest performance she had ever seen. And she was a very cultured woman."

"Well, perhaps you should put your acting skills to use with Morris."

"Somehow, I don't think he'd share my grandmother's opinion." He chuckled then sighed in exasperation. "I've got to give him something. And soon."

"I'll work on Vince, but I can't rush it and I can't promise anything." I said. "But I may have a way of making inroads with Ellie Penner."

***

I saw Ellie hurrying toward class and I rushed to catch up with her.

"Good morning," I said when I reached her side.

She smiled but said nothing.

"Listen," I said, "I've been thinking about your audition."

"Ms. James," she said, her pace slowing, "I know you think it's a bad idea, but I'm not going to change my mind."

"Yes, I do think it's a bad idea. That's why I want to take you." She stopped and looked at me with wide eyes. "I'll drive you to your audition. I can get you to and from Toronto much faster than the bus. I can probably even get you back here in time for your last class. And you won't be wandering around the city alone."

"Oh my goodness," she said, throwing her arms around my neck. "Thank you!"

I hoped if I could get Ellie alone for an extended period of time, I would be able to get some answers to the questions Jeffers and I had been banging our heads against the wall trying to solve.

"I still think you should let your dad know," I said as gently as possible.

"I can't," she said, releasing the embrace.

"He may surprise you, Ellie. He might be much more understanding than you think."

I flashed back to the happy family photo. Deep down, the Armin Penner in that picture still had to exist.

"Ms. James, if that's the condition of you driving me, I'll take the bus," Ellie said and started back down the hall.

"It's not," I said, falling into step next to her. Her pace quickened, and I struggled to keep up. "I will take you."

She stopped. "You won't tell my dad?"

"No."

"Promise?"

"Ellie, I promise, but—"

She started to walk away again. I put my hand on her arm and she stopped with her back to me.

"I know this is important to you," I said.

"It's everything to me."

"That's why I want to help you." She turned and looked me straight in the eye. I went on. "The audition process is a long one—if you make it past the first round. I don't want you taking it on by yourself. I know you think it's just as simple as getting on a bus, but there's a lot more to it than that. You can't just skip school and leave town without anyone knowing where you're going." She lowered her eyes and I saw her shoulders sag. "You're seventeen, Ellie. You're still a minor. If you don't show up for class, the school will call your father. What are you going to tell him then?"

"I…"

"And I could get into a lot of trouble for taking you out of town without permission. So we need to figure something out, okay? Something that protects both of us."

"Ms. James, I can tell him something so he knows I'd be missing school, but it can't be the truth."

"Ellie, I don't understand—"

"No, you don't, Ms. James. How could you? Have you ever had everything in your life taken away from you?" I had, but this moment was not about me. "I want this. I want it so bad I can taste it. And I'm going to do whatever it takes."

"Ellie—"

"Thank you for your offer, Ms. James, but I don't need your help." She clutched her books close to her chest and hurried off down the hall.

Armin Penner had implemented strict family changes after Adele died. It was clear Ellie was not committed to the conversion. I wondered if Armin Penner himself had bought in completely or if the changes were more a product of grief than anything else like Paul had suggested. If that was the case, there was a chance of Ellie and her father eventually finding common ground. But only if they could holster their tempers. And their judgment.

I followed Ellie's path to class and passed a bulletin board where a memorial had been set up for Al Macie. In the centre was a framed photo surrounded by more candid pictures of him that had obviously been added by students and staff. People had started to pin pieces of paper with messages of condolence, cherished memories, and funny stories.

"It grows a little more every day."

I turned to find Principal Harvey standing just behind me.

I smiled. "It's lovely."

"He was very well liked," Gerald Harvey said. "It took a while for everyone to warm up to him because of his...well, you know. But, still, he was one of our most popular teachers."

This was the second time Al Macie's sexuality had been brought up as the one thing that made him only generally well liked rather than wholly. Jeffers had mentioned it after he had interviewed the staff.

"Mr. Harvey, is there anyone, in particular, who had trouble with Mr. Macie's sexuality?"

"Ms. James." He said it as a warning that I should keep my voice down.

"I'm sorry," I said looking around at the nearby students, none of whom seemed to be taking any interest in our conversation. And I doubted any one of them would care even if they had been. But I heeded the warning and went on. "It's just that I find it so sad, in this day and age, that one's ... lifestyle ... is still under such criticism."

"That's because you're in the theatre, Ms. James."

"I don't think that has anything to do with it. It's—"

A commotion started up somewhere down the hall. In five huge strides, Gerald Harvey was between two boys with a finger pointed at each of their chests and was uttering something I couldn't hear. I saw both boys adopt attitude and throw blame before heading to the office, the large mass of Gerald Harvey looming over them.

I turned back to the memorial. To Al Macie's kind face and warm eyes. "Who did this to you?" I whispered. I was answered only by more questions.

Could Vincent Leduc have been carrying around a wrong done to him years ago, carefully planning payback? If Armin Penner was indeed firm in his new beliefs of the Old Order and knew of his daughter's planned defection from the faith, how far would he go to stop it? What did Ellie mean by "whatever it takes"? And there was something else. Something new. There was something about the fact that Al Macie was only "generally" well liked that made me wonder if we'd been looking in entirely the wrong direction.

Chapter 14

Three texts to Jeffers went unanswered and his phone went right to voice mail when I tried to call. I had an hour before I needed to be at rehearsal and my mind was racing. Against my better judgment I found myself dialing Glynn Radley's number. He picked up on the fourth ring.

"I'm so sorry to bother you," I said. "Is now a good time?"

"I'm waiting to get in to see the vet. Edith is off the yams. Hasn't eaten in two days. I don't know what to do."

"Do you mind if I come wait with you?"

"Be my guest."

Glynn was sitting on the front stoop of the clinic when I arrived. Edith was lying next him. She raised her eyes when I approached but didn't look like she had the energy to manage much else.

"I've never seen her like this," Glynn said. "I didn't know dogs could get depressed."

"I think they feel things much more deeply than we realize," I said. "Of course, it might be something else altogether. It's good you're having her looked at." I crouched down and stroked the dog's head. "Why aren't you inside?"

"They wouldn't let us in. The girl met us at the door in a haz-mat suit and asked if we could wait out here."

"A haz-mat suit?"

"Well, not really. But she was all covered up. Opened the door just enough to talk and barely even that."

"That doesn't sound good."

"She said it shouldn't be much longer, so I doubt it's anything serious. What did you want to talk about?"

I sat down on the other side of the Great Dane. "I want to ask about whether Al ever mentioned having trouble with anyone at work regarding his ... your ... relationship."

"Because we're gay?"

I nodded.

He shook his head. "I wouldn't use the word 'trouble.'"

"But there was something?"

"You have to understand, this is a pretty religious town. I'm not saying homophobic. I'm saying that homosexuality is not something a lot of people here grew up with. I think it's still new for a lot of people. Something not everyone understands. Or is comfortable with."

"So?"

"Al was always very respectful. And careful. He tried to keep his personal life personal. Everybody knew, of course, but he chose to keep it out of the workplace as much as possible." He paused, taking a moment to stroke the length of the large dog beside him. "It's still not easy. Being gay in this world. I'm not out at the firehouse. The boys think Al is short for Alison. I don't know that they'd have trouble with the truth, to be fair, but it's easier just to let them think what they want." Another pause. "What's this about, Bella?"

"It's probably nothing. But it's been implied that there might have been someone on staff at the school who may have been less than accepting of Al's sexuality. I'm wondering if he ever mentioned anyone to you."

"What are you saying? You think Al's death was a hate crime now?"

"No! No." In the back of my mind, I could see Jeffers wagging a finger at me for getting poor Glynn all worked up over a cockamamie theory that likely had nothing to do with anything. "I'm sorry. I don't want to upset you. I just want to be sure we've covered everything as far as Al's death is concerned. And if there is someone—"

"There are a lot of someones. Bella, things have changed over the years, yes. People and organizations have become much more progressive and diverse. But there are still a lot of old boys' clubs out there and the education system is a big one. Al played the game for years. Manipulated his personality so people wouldn't guess. Endured dinner after dinner given by well-meaning colleagues as a means of introducing him to their female friends. Going to gay bars in the States because he was petrified local people would find out. And when he finally did come out, there were golf tournaments, fundraisers, other work events where he bit his tongue as people around him said fag instead of cigarette and remarked on what queer weather we'd been having. It was a constant struggle for Al. Don't get me wrong; he was out and he was proud. He didn't hide who he was anymore and he'd made some wonderful friends at work, but he always knew it was more comfortable for everyone when he kept his personal details … quiet. The effort was conscious, you know?"

"Mr. Radley?" The door opened behind us and a vet tech stuck her head out. "Sorry to keep you waiting. You and Edith can come in now. Oh, hi, Bella."

"Hi, Stephanie," I said, getting up and following Glynn and Edith inside. "What's going on? Is everything okay?"

She was in the process of removing full-body coveralls made out of some rubbery material. I could see one of the other vet techs doing the same behind the front desk.

"Oh yes, fine," she said smiling. "Brimstone was in for his annual physical. We don't like to take any chances. One year he got loose and we … let's just say we weren't prepared. Want me to let Paul know you're here?"

"Thanks."

"Sure thing. Mr. Radley, we'll be right with you," she said and disappeared into the back room.

"Brimstone?" Glynn asked.

"The meanest cat in the world," I said. "I don't understand how he puts up with it."

"Because of Laura," the girl at the front desk said.

"I'm sorry?"

"Brimstone was Laura's cat."

"Who's Laura?"

"I have no idea!"

"He's never mentioned her to you?"

"No!" I was on the phone with my best friend, Natalie, during a break from rehearsal. "And before you ask, no, he doesn't have a sister."

"Cousin, maybe?"

"Natalie!"

"What? I'm just going through all the possibilities before we jump to the obvious."

"That she's an ex?"

"That seems the most likely."

"But why hasn't he mentioned her? We've had enough conversations about that damn cat you'd think he would have said something."

Natalie and I had met years before when we were both at university in Montreal. She had become more of a sister than a friend and the only person who had known me at my very worst and still managed to love me.

"Maybe it ended badly," she said.

"Then why does he still have her cat?"

"Maybe that's his punishment."

I laughed out loud in spite of my mood. "I just don't understand why he'd hide this."

"Have you told him about all your exes?"

"I don't have 'exes.' I have one significant ex. And no."

"Hmmm."

"Not because I'm hiding anything!" I said. "There's just nothing worth mentioning." I checked the time. I had to get back. "Brimstone is the cat from hell. And Paul loves him. Which means he must have loved her."

"And now he loves you."

"Then why has he kept this from me?"

"Talk to him."

"I don't want to be one of those insecure girlfriends…"

"Then don't be. It's not like Laura's a secret. The girl at the clinic knew."

"I know, but—"

"You are going to drive yourself crazy wondering. And I'm going to have to listen to you. So, for my sake, talk to him."

I told her I would. And I knew I should. But I wasn't sure I could.

"You okay?" Paul asked later that evening. "You're awfully quiet."

He joined me on the couch, stretched out on his back, and put his head in my lap. Moustache jumped on top of him and curled up on his shins.

"I'm fine," I said. To prove it, I rattled on about my morning with the students, my alienation of Ellie, and Jeffers' labelling of Vincent Leduc as a psychopath. I told him about how Eeyore had actually told a joke in rehearsal and how Manda Rogers had seemingly moved on from Powell and set her sights on the director of *Juno and the Paycock* who was visiting from Ireland. I talked about everything and anything, except what I really wanted to talk about.

"Maybe he'll take her back to Ireland when his contract's over."

Paul had been on the receiving end of Manda's wiles the previous season, but had managed to resist succumbing to them. Another reason she had it out for me.

"From your lips…" I said.

I stroked his hair. The scent of his shampoo met my nose and I leaned down to kiss his forehead. He took my hands in his own, kissed each one in turn, then held them against his chest. I wondered if he had sat like this with Laura. He must have sensed the shift in my psyche because he asked again whether I was all right.

"Actually, there is something I'd like to ask you about."

"I knew it," he said, proud of himself.

He kissed my hands again.

"This afternoon," I started slowly, hating the insecurities that were taking over, "when I was at the clinic, one of the girls mentioned—"

My phone rang. Jeffers.

"I'm sorry," I said, reaching for the phone.

Paul sat up. Moustache snorted at the interruption.

"That's okay. Take your time. I'm going to make us some popcorn."

At the mention of popcorn, Moustache's ears twitched. He leapt off the couch and ran into the kitchen, skidding as he rounded the corner.

"Sorry I'm so late getting back to you," Jeffers said when I'd answered. "There was a torso floating in the Niagara River. What's up?"

"A torso?" It amazed me how Jeffers could be so nonchalant when discussing the discovery of random body parts.

"Happens more often than you'd think. So…?"

I launched into the details of my exchange with Ellie.

"Ballsy move, Samuel. If you want to get arrested for kidnapping."

"I said I wouldn't take her without permission."

"Best find another way altogether. Even if she tells you she cleared it with her dad, she'll probably be lying. You can get in a lot of trouble."

"I know if I can just get some time alone with her, I could get her to talk."

"Whatever you come up with, make sure it's above board or Morris will have our heads. Anything else?"

I mentioned my conversation with Gerald Harvey. Then told him of my meeting with Glynn.

"I wish you hadn't said anything to him. The guy is barely hanging on."

"I know. I'm sorry. I thought I might be able to learn something that could help."

"And did you?"

"No," I said. "Well, that's not entirely true. But nothing that pertained directly to the case. When you interviewed the staff, you said you got the feeling not everyone was accepting of Al's being gay. Was there anyone specific?"

"I'd have to check my notes, but I'm sure I was just picking up on the kind of vibe Glynn was talking about."

"It seems strange to me, that's all. First you commented on it, then Harvey. What if it's more than just discomfort? What if someone really had a problem with Al's sexuality?"

"And killed him because of it? That'd be some problem."

"It wouldn't be the first time."

Jeffers let out a sigh. "Let me go back over my notes. See if anything stands out."

"Thanks."

"Don't hold your breath."

By the time Paul returned with the popcorn, a large bowl for the two of us and a smaller, unbuttered bowl for Moustache, I realized holding my breath was exactly what I was doing.

"You know he doesn't like it plain," I said.

"He'll get enough butter from our fingers. Everything okay with Jeffers?"

"Fine," I said, tossing a kernel at the dog, who caught it midair.

"So ... you were saying?"

"I was?"

"One of the girls mentioned...?"

"Do you want some wine?" I asked, getting up.

"Bells, stop stalling," he said, taking my hand and coaxing me back down onto the couch. "What is it?"

"It's nothing. I'm just being silly."

"It's obviously not nothing. To you."

I looked into his eyes. His face. He took my breath away. I was amazed that someone like him would ever look twice at someone like me. Natalie was right when she'd said he loved me. I knew that. And she was also right when she said I would drive myself crazy with worry if I didn't come right out and ask him about Laura.

"That whole thing with Brimstone … One of the girls mentioned he had belonged to someone named Laura?"

He wiped his hands on a napkin, got up, and walked out of the room.

Chapter 15

He returned with a glass of red in one hand and a Jack Daniels in the other. He only drank Jack when he needed to unwind from something particularly difficult, so I knew which way the conversation was going to go.

He set the wine on the coffee table, threw some popcorn for the dog, and took a long haul from his glass before sitting down next to me.

"Laura was my fiancée," he said.

I looked to the glass of wine but thought better of it.

He went on. "She died four years ago."

"Paul, I'm sorry."

"No, I'm sorry. I should have told you. It's hard for me to talk about."

"I understand," I said, taking his free hand. "We don't have to do this."

"No," he said, "I want to." He took another sip but remained silent.

"How did she die?" I asked, gently.

"She killed herself." I went for the wine. "She'd tried to before. A couple of times. But someone always found her."

"Paul, I…"

"She wasn't a happy person. Laura. She was good at disguising it. Those who didn't know her well thought she was happy enough, but…" he shook his head. "She'd been on medication her whole life. The first time she attempted suicide she was only twelve. Can you believe that?"

I remained silent, soaking it all in, waiting for him to continue. He didn't.

"How long had you been together?" I asked.

"Seven years." My heart fell into my stomach. "She'd only tried it once while we were dating. I found her in the bathtub with her wrists cut."

"Paul, we really don't need to talk about this if you—"

He grabbed my hand and held on tight.

"They never found her body," he said. "She finally managed to do it without anyone finding her and stopping it."

I flashed back to my conversation with Jeffers about the torso in the river and his words, *"Happens more often than you'd think."*

"How do you know she—"

"There was a note."

"I'm so sorry," I said. "What that must have been like for you. What it must still be like."

"What's important is that she's finally at peace. And so is her family." He ran his hand through my hair and cradled my face. "And so am I." He drained his glass and set it down on the table. "But poor Brimstone ... I don't think he'll ever recover. Maine Coons are fiercely loyal to their humans and he was devoted to Laura. When she died, it's like a switch was flipped. He turned from this lovable, playful, kittenlike cat to ... well, the cat he is now. I think he feels like she abandoned him. And she did, I guess. She did all of us."

"So you won't abandon him."

"Nope. Not for anything."

***

I woke in the middle of the night to the sound of my phone vibrating. Paul's arms were around me and his breath was warm on my neck. I untangled myself from his embrace as stealthily as possible, wrapped myself in a blanket, and took the phone into the hall.

"I think I may have something." Jeffers said before I'd even had a chance to say "hello."

"It better be life-threatening."

"What? That's not very nice."

"It's four in the morning!"

"Is it?"

I could hear the baby screaming in the background. The perfect child had finally discovered his lungs, it seemed.

"Sorry," he said. "I couldn't sleep and decided to get some work done. I had no idea how late it was. Or early, I guess. Anyway, now that I have you—"

"Can this really not wait?"

"No. And besides, you're not going to be able to go back to sleep now. You're going to be thinking about why I called. Forming all kinds of theories in your head. Driving yourself crazy with assumptions and wishing you had—"

"All right!" I said and stumbled downstairs to put the kettle on. "Is this about the staff? Did you look through your notes?"

"I did, but there's nothing."

"Hmmm." I wasn't entirely surprised, but I wasn't ready to write it off yet. I said as much to Jeffers.

"Fine. But I'm not calling about that."

"Okay?"

"Okay, so, Leduc and Macie were classmates at the University of Alberta. I managed to track down one of their teachers. Brian Dayleward. Still teaching if you can believe it! Seventy-five years old!"

"Go on," I said through a yawn.

"Dayleward said the two of them were best friends until their final year. Then they barely spoke to one another. He couldn't even get them to work together in class."

"Does the teacher know what happened?"

"Thinks it had something to do with an accident that occurred during the summer. Leduc's sister died. Said Vince was pretty despondent for much of the last year. Shut everyone out."

"But Al in particular?"

"That's what he said."

The kettle started to whistle.

"How did she die?" I asked, setting my tea to steep.

"Drugs, evidently. I've got a call in to a buddy on the Edmonton force. Hopefully I'll be able to learn a little bit more about the case. All I could find were a couple of old news reports that said very little. Just that a girl died at a house party of an apparent drug overdose."

"Any suspicion of foul play or anything?"

"Nope. Just kids messing around and being stupid."

"They were hardly kids. They must have been in their early twenties," I said.

"Girl was eighteen."

"Still old enough to know better."

"Yep."

"All right," I said, taking my tea into the living room and curling up on the sofa, "so we know Vince's sister died from an overdose at a party. We don't know if Al Macie was at the party or was any way involved."

"I think it's safe to assume he was. On both counts. Otherwise, why would Leduc have ended the friendship?"

"Grief."

"But if they were best friends, wouldn't it make sense that he would turn to him for comfort?"

"There are no rules with grief, Jeffers. Everyone handles it in their own unique way," I said, thinking of my own experience. Of Paul's. Of Glynn Radley's and Armin Penner's. Grief comes in all shapes and sizes and doesn't discriminate. Like a snowflake, it's never the same.

"No. If Leduc has been obsessed with Macie all these years, it's got to stem from whatever happened that night. Hopefully, I'll hear from my buddy soon."

"Wait a minute. Glynn said Al and Vince had never been friends. Remember?"

There was an audible exhale from Jeffers. "So you think Al deliberately kept the incident and the truth about his relationship with Vince a secret?"

"Maybe."

"Why? It doesn't make any sense. We need to talk to Glynn."

"What about Vince?"

"Him too. He just got a whole lot more interesting."

A crash jolted me awake. For the second time in only a few hours my sleep was disturbed and I cursed the day ahead as I knew it was going to be a tough one to get through. I'd fallen asleep on the couch. Paul appeared in the kitchen doorway.

"Watch where you step." Paul said. He was bent over, picking up pieces of broken glass from the kitchen floor. "I'm so sorry." He held out the handle of what was once a juice pitcher. "It just slipped."

"That's okay. It was cheap. And I didn't really like it."

Orange juice pooled around his feet. Moustache had his

nose pressed up against the window of the back door, looking in from outside and brimming with curiosity about what had fallen on the floor. And whether he could eat it.

"You all right to clean this up?" I asked. "I'll run out and get us some more juice."

Paul nodded, then called after me, "And something to put it in."

While the Avondale boasted a one-stop shopping experience, its selection of pitchers was lacking. They were plastic, which in light of the current situation, seemed like a good thing. Of the two options I had, one was yellow with sunflowers and the other was green with frogs. As I played a mental game of eeny meeny miny moe, Leland Penner entered the store with a friend. I grabbed the jug closest to me, ducked my head, and moved quickly toward the cash.

"You're that woman. From the school. You were talking to my sister," he said, cutting me off at the pass.

"I'm sorry. I think you have me—"

"And you were at the house, too. With that detective."

I opened my mouth to speak, but words failed me. I held on tightly to the frogs while my insides turned to jelly in the presence of this fifteen-year-old boy.

"You police?" he asked.

"I work with Detective Jeffers occasionally," I stammered.

"You guys found who killed that teacher?"

"I'm afraid I can't discuss—"

He snickered. Cockiness oozed out of every pore and made me wonder just what he thought he'd gotten away with.

"Got what he deserved, if you ask me," he said, knocking my shoulder as he brushed by me. The frogs went tumbling to the floor.

"Why would you say that?" I asked.

He turned back to face me. "Karma's a bitch. Isn't that what they say?"

"I don't see what karma has to do with anything in this case."

"Don't you? I bet my mother would beg to differ."

"What does that mean?" Jeffers asked sleepily.

"I have no idea!"

"Well, when you figure it out, let me know. I'm going back to bed."

"Oh, no you don't! Not after last night. You're going to talk to me whether you like it or not."

I heard the rustling of blankets and the odd grunt before Jeffers' begrudging, "Fine."

"All this time, Jeffers, all this time we've been thinking Armin Penner killed Macie because of his involvement with Ellie—"

"Yes, and now we're thinking Leduc killed Macie because he was somehow responsible for the death of his sister."

"Let me finish," I said, overlapping. "Wait a minute. What did you just say?"

"I said, the focus has shifted to Leduc because—"

"Oh my god!"

"What?"

"Do you still have Adele Penner's hospital records?"

"Yeah."

"I need to see them. I'm coming over. But first I have a stop to make."

Chapter 16

I found Powell Avery tucked in the back of the rehearsal hall watching a scene from *On the Rocks*. He only had a small role in the play but was understudying one of the leads so he was there taking notes.

"Ah, I heard a rumour you were in this show," he teased.

I had yet to enjoy the camaraderie of the rest of the company, as I'd only been called for rehearsals requiring myself and my illustrious scene partner, the poster boy for doom and gloom.

"How's it going, by the way?" he asked, nodding his head slightly in the direction of Robert Cole, who was whining to the director about something.

I rolled my eyes, and Powell smiled empathetically.

"What are you doing here? Why aren't you singing and dancing and taking off your clothes?"

"Very funny," I said. "Oddly, I have the day off."

"How did you manage that?"

"I think it's probably an oversight, so I'm going to make a run for it before they figure it out. Before I do, though, do you have a minute?" I asked.

We retreated to the corridor.

"Do you remember, the other day, we were talking

about Adele Penner's death?" He nodded. "You mentioned there was a doctor named in the lawsuit and that you'd been dating her brother. It was Al Macie, wasn't it?"

"I was going to say something when we were talking, but we got cut off. I still can't believe he's gone. When I heard about his death…" He shook his head, unable to put words to his thoughts. "I mean, we dated on and off for a while. I probably shouldn't even use the word 'date.' It was really more like hooking up, but somehow that sounds so … cheap and cavalier and it wasn't that."

"Did you know Al was in a relationship?"

"Yeah. I think he and Glynn had some kind of understanding. I never really asked."

"You mean an open relationship?"

"Not quite. That implies that a couple can pursue other intimate relationships outside of their primary relationship. I don't think Al or Glynn was interested in that."

"So, just sex then?"

Powell laughed and ran his fingers though his hair. "No, but … It's hard to explain."

"It's okay. You don't need to get into it. I get it. I think." Powell looked relieved. "Did Glynn know?"

"I don't know, to be honest. We'd usually meet if Glynn was working a weekend. Head out of town."

"You mean it's been going on all this time?"

"Occasionally. The odd weekend. Do you mind if I ask—?"

"What this is all about?" I finished for him.

I filled Powell in on my relationship with Jeffers and the Niagara Regional Police and my current involvement in Al Macie's case.

"You think there might be a link between Adele Penner's death and Al's?"

"I really can't say. And I would be very grateful if you kept this conversation between the two of us."

"Of course," he said. "Al didn't talk much about the lawsuit. He'd mentioned it and spoke briefly about how it was tearing his sister apart but … They hadn't been close for some time and I know he wanted to reach out to her. I don't know if he ever did." He moved toward the door of the rehearsal hall then stopped. "Al was … amazing," he said. "If there's anything I can do…"

"Thanks. This has been very helpful." He turned to go. "Powell," I said, "what was his sister's name? Did he ever mention it?"

"Jayne Evans," Jeffers said. We were standing in his kitchen with Adele's medical records and the little Jeffers had been able to find pertaining to the lawsuit spread out on the counter and small kitchen table. "There are a couple of other doctors named here too, but she fits the age. It's got to be her. But, wait a minute, if Al was having an affair and Glynn found out, that's a motive. We need to talk to Glynn again."

"Powell said they had an understanding."

"Powell said he *thought* they had an understanding. That's what you said."

"Okay, but—"

"Bella, if there was an understanding, and Glynn knew all about Al's infidelity, then maybe there's no issue. But if there wasn't…"

"Then we're destroying the very foundation his life was based on," I said. "You've seen him, Jeffers. You know how much be loved Al. And, yeah, maybe Al was a cheating bastard, but to Glynn, he was the love of his life. I don't want to take that away from him. He's lost so much."

Jeffers and I stared at one another from our opposing sides.

"He didn't kill Al, Jeffers."

"You don't know that."

"I do. I know Morris is breathing down your neck for a resolution, but I think deep down you know it too."

Jeffers sighed. "I'll drop it. For now. But I am not letting it go."

"Thank you. Now what else have we got on Al's sister?"

"Armin Penner went after her hard," Jeffers said.

I looked over Jeffers' shoulder at the file. "Looks like he placed most of the blame for Adele's death solely on her. No wonder it almost tore her apart."

Jeffers put the file down and phoned in a request to someone at the police department for any information about Ms. Evans to be emailed to him as soon as possible.

"Says here Adele went into anaphylactic shock just minutes after being put under," I said. "Must have been something in the anaesthesia."

"Something to ask our doctor."

"Do you really think Macie's death was an act of vengeance? It just seems so … I don't know. I mean, there was no premeditation."

"The murder itself wasn't premeditated. That doesn't mean whatever confrontation led up to it wasn't."

"I guess."

"What is it? You seem troubled."

"It's nothing really. It's just that a couple of days ago, Al Macie was a popular teacher, beloved partner, arts advocate, and now he's been having affairs, keeping secrets from his partner, and has been linked to the deaths of two women … I feel like the Al Macie we thought we knew is only a fraction of the man he really was."

"I can't comment on the affairs or secrets, but as far as the women go, he didn't kill them, Samuel. 'Linked' is too strong a word here. Vince's sister's death was ruled accidental. And in Adele Penner's case, he's only guilty by association. He wasn't even there. Probably didn't even know the woman."

"I know all that. I do. But people have held grudges against him, Jeffers, for years it seems. Vince, the Penners. Who else might there be?

"Hopefully no one," Jeffers said and knocked on the kitchen table. "I've got my hands full with this case. The last thing I need is another suspect." Jeffers' phone chirped. He swiped the screen. "Jayne Evans lives in Port Dalhousie. Care to come for a ride?"

"Sure."

Jeffers did a quick tidy up of the kitchen. I didn't move from my place at the table.

"Is there something else?" he asked.

I went through some quick mental aerobics in which I contemplated asking Jeffers to check the police database for information about Laura. However, when I got to the part where I realized I had no last name, no real timeline, and no physical description, I concluded I ultimately had no business pursuing it any further.

"I'm good. Let's go," I said, gathering my things, heading for the door.

"You're sure?"

I wasn't, but I nodded anyway. If there was more to Laura's story, I'd get it from Paul. In his own time. In the meantime, there was Al Macie's story to deal with. And I felt we'd really only begun to scratch the surface.

***

I'd never been to Port Dalhousie in spite of its being less than a half hour from Niagara-on-the-Lake and boasting the area's most popular beach and a downtown core that was built for nightlife. Jeffers regaled me with stories from his wilder days when beach-bumming and bar-hopping were the thing and picking up girls was the goal.

He drove past a structure that was artistically and purposefully boarded up. "There's an antique carousel in there. It only runs in the summer. Five cents a ride. Been there almost a hundred years and the price has never gone up," Jeffers said, as part of a brief tour of the community. "And that's where I met Aria," he said, pointing out a pub at a corner where the downtown seemed to end and the residential area began.

"The Kilt and Clover?"

"Warm Beer & Lousy Food," Jeffers said with a smile I didn't understand. "It's their motto."

"Sounds appealing."

"It's great. Really. Aria was working there one summer. Used to pour me full pints but only charged me for halves. All the girls wear these short kilts … The place is an institution. I bet Paul has some stories."

"I'm sure he does."

Whatever it was about girls in short kilts, it had a universal effect on men. It wouldn't have surprised me at all to learn that Paul had tipped back many a glass there in his day.

Jeffers manoeuvred the car down a number of small streets, challenging my sense of direction, before pulling into the driveway of a large, plantationesque house with an open porch wrapping around the main level and a screened-in porch up above. The house's green trim was made all the more vibrant by the white siding, which also had the same effect on the pristinely landscaped front lawn. It looked downright lush in spite of the fact we were in the middle of a mucky spring. A red Volvo, which Jeffers informed me was an 875RUO 1963 P1800 coupe, occupied the driveway—and Jeffers' attention.

I rang the doorbell and offered our names to the woman who answered.

"Are you a collector?" she asked Jeffers, who had circled around to the back of the car and was peering in through the rear window.

"Sorry, ma'am." Jeffers said, straightening up and hurrying to the front door. "Just an admirer. Jayne Evans?" The woman nodded. "Detective Sergeant Andre Jeffers."

"Your partner has already said," she said with a smile. She was older than Al. But there was no mistaking they were siblings. She had the same dark hair and fine features. She was slender and exuded the same warmth her brother had. "She's my husband's pride and joy. Brings her out as soon as the snow's gone. We get a lot of people stopping to look at her."

"She's a beauty." Jeffers said, looking wistfully at the car. "My uncle had a white one. Like the one Roger Moore drove in *The Saint*. Used to take me out whenever we'd visit. I loved that car. It—" I cleared my throat as a cue to focus on the task at hand. "Sorry. I get excited."

"That's all right." Jayne said, and she welcomed us inside.

We settled in the living room after declining an offer of refreshment. Family photos filled the shelves. Jayne with her husband. Three girls, who I assumed to be her daughters, showing off varying degrees of athletic prowess. And a few photographs of a much younger Jayne in an army uniform.

"You're ex-military?" I asked.

She followed my eyes to where the pictures sat in their frames. "Yes. I was a doctor during Desert Storm. It's where I met Jason. He's a nurse and in typical fashion, or stereotypical, I guess, one thing led to another." She chuckled. "In addition to medicine, I speak seven languages and love to travel. I figured the military would give me a chance to combine all three of my passions."

"You just did the one tour?"

"I got pregnant shortly after we returned home. Jason spent some time in Somalia, but I never went back. I don't imagine you're here to discuss my military history. I'm assuming this has to do with Al?"

"Actually, no," Jeffers said. "We're here on another matter. But first, please let me express our condolences."

"Thank you," Jayne said. "Al and I hadn't seen in each other in several years. It really feels no different now that he's gone."

"If you don't mind my asking," I said, "did you and Al have a falling out?"

"No, nothing like that. What is it they say? You can't choose your family?"

"Something along those lines."

"Al was my brother and I loved him, but two more different people never walked the face of this earth," she said matter-of-factly. "We were never particularly close as children, and as we grew older, we grew further apart. There was no great feud or family drama. We just never were able to relate to one another." I nodded my understanding. "Have there been any developments with his case?"

Jeffers shook his head. "Nothing we can talk too much about."

"Of course. So if it's not Al, what brings you by?"

"We'd like to talk to you about Adele Penner," Jeffers said.

Jayne took a deep breath and held it for several moments before letting it out. "There's a name I hoped I'd never hear again."

"I'm sorry, Dr. Evans. I know it was a difficult time."

"I was accused of murder, Detective. I was ultimately cleared of all suspicion, but it nearly cost me everything. My job, my marriage, my reputation. Not to mention the emotional toll it took on me. On my whole family." She was silent for a time. The sound of her deep breathing filled the room. Finally she put her shoulders back and looked Jeffers straight in the eye. "I will answer whatever questions you have, but before I do, may I ask why this case is coming up again after all these years?"

Jeffers hesitated. We were about to ask this woman to relive one of the most painful times of her life. She deserved to know why. She may have been ex-military and she may have been strong enough to rise above the accusations of Armin Penner, but I wasn't sure she'd be able to handle the news that she may have been indirectly responsible for her brother's death.

Jayne Evans was silent as Jeffers connected the dots between Al and Adele Penner. When he'd finished, she buried her head in her hands and stayed that way for several moments.

"Dr. Evans, according to the lawsuit, Armin Penner seemed to hold you almost entirely accountable for his wife's death. Of all the people in the room with her that day, why single you out?"

"Because I was the one who gave her the drug."

Chapter 17

"I'm an anaesthesiologist. And I was the one administering the anaesthetic to Adele that day. We always ask patients about allergies to any medications when we take their history. Most patients have never had the meds before, so how would they know? Do you know if you're allergic to rocuronium?" Jeffers and I both shook our heads. "Exactly. It happens. It happens more than it should. And until there is a better way of screening medications, it will continue to happen. There is simply no way of knowing."

"Can you talk us briefly through what happened with Mrs. Penner?" Jeffers asked.

Jayne sighed audibly and tears sprang to her eyes. "She was a lovely woman," she said. "I remember her husband was driving her crazy with his worrying. She had a wonderful way of teasing him yet being able to comfort him at the same time. It was a routine surgery. But no matter how minor the procedure, there are always risks. We never make promises. Still, no one expected Adele Penner to do anything other than walk out of the hospital a few hours later a little lighter for the removal of a kidney stone."

"What happened once you were in the O.R.?"

"It was so fast. Everything happened so fast," Jayne said, her eyes looking at something a million miles away.

"I administered the anaesthetic and the reaction was almost instantaneous. We are prepared for this, Detective. As I said, it happens. We immediately gave epinephrine. The patient … Mrs. Penner didn't respond and was in full cardiac arrest within moments."

"I thought epinephrine was kind of foolproof," I said.

"Have you ever heard of Hypertrophic Obstructive Cardiomyopathy?"

"No."

"The treatment can be worse than the problem. The epinephrine causes the heart to fail, and as a result—"

"Cannot counter the anaphylaxis," I finished. Jayne Evans nodded. "And Adele Penner had this hypertro—?"

"HOCM. There was nothing in her medical history, but it's likely it simply hadn't been diagnosed yet. And maybe it wouldn't have been. She hadn't complained of any symptoms as far as I knew."

"So it was a combination of the allergic reaction and the heart condition," Jeffers said.

Again Jayne nodded. "We did everything we could. But sometimes…" Jayne took a moment. "We weren't surprised when the lawsuit came. It was supposed to have been an in-and-out surgery. What happened was against all odds. What *did* surprise us was how far things went. The venom with which Armin Penner attacked. 'Malpractice' is a well-known word in the medical profession. One that no one takes lightly but one that is commonly used all the same. 'Murder,' on the other hand…"

"Can you be more specific?"

"More specific than a murder accusation?"

"More specific about why Armin Penner might have felt that was just?"

"Why, Detective? He had just lost his wife to routine surgery. To a series of complications that would have been entirely avoidable *if* we had only known about things that were impossible to know." Jayne heaved a heavy sigh. "He didn't believe those things had happened. The allergic reaction. The pre-existing heart condition. He thought we had made it all up to cover our own asses. To cover up our negligence."

"Dr. Evans, we know there was a settlement. If Adele's cause of death was the result of a series of natural, albeit unforeseen, circumstances, why would there have been a payout? Isn't that an admission of wrongdoing?" Jeffers asked.

"Whether it is or not, these kinds of accusations are damning to reputations, to credibility, to funding … the reach is astonishing. Professionally. Personally. If a few dollars can make everything go away, it's a small price to pay."

"But it didn't go away for Armin Penner. Adele's life wasn't a small price." Jeffers said.

"You know that's not what I meant."

Jeffers nodded. "I'm sorry."

Jayne rose from her seat, crossed to one of the two large windows in the room, and stood looking out for some time.

"I gave the drug, so I became his target," she said, finally, her back to us. "I was the one he went after the hardest."

"In what way?" I asked.

"For starters, he claimed the education I'd received in the army was not equal to that achieved in more traditional universities. He had all of my records and transcripts ordered for review. He called into question the qualifications of my professors. He put a blight on the whole program. Or tried to. And then when that didn't work, he..." She brought a hand to her mouth and bowed her head.

"Jayne?" I asked. "Are you all right?"

"He claimed I was depressed. Suffering from PTSD. That I had some kind of death wish and was a danger to myself and my patients."

Jeffers flipped through his notes. "Were you diagnosed with—?"

"No!" She turned to face us. "He was grasping at straws. Pulling out anything he could think of that's associated with military history. Anything that might make me the guilty party. That might explain his wife's death. And to satisfy him, I was subjected to numerous psychological reviews and was suspended from my job pending the outcome of these. People I worked with, friends, began to look at me as if maybe, deep down, I had harboured this secret. Old patients came out of the woodwork, questioning procedures I had worked on and wondering if, somehow, I was to blame for the tiniest of issues." She paused. "I went along with all of it. I knew Adele's death had been clean so I cooperated. For as long as I could. Finally, mercifully, my chief shut the whole thing down and insisted the hospital offer a settlement to the family."

Jeffers and I sat in a stunned silence as the scope of Armin Penner's grief circled us, watched us, dared us. It wondered whether we would measure its behaviour against its loss and declare its actions justified or see it as vindictive and calculating.

Images of Penner began floating through my mind. Him in his straw hat and suspenders, holding the weight of the day's labour on his shoulders. Him with Adele, clean-shaven, smiling, their whole life ahead of them. I thought about how I'd handled my own heartache after my parents died. The pain I'd caused and the blame I'd sought. I could certainly understand his anguish. His need to hold someone accountable. To have answers even when there aren't any.

"So," said Jayne Evans, "you think he is still seeking vengeance. Trying to get to me through Al? I took someone he loved, so he…"

"We don't know, ma'am," Jeffers said.

"But it's possible?"

"All the evidence proves Al's death was the result of an argument that got out of hand. Whoever killed him didn't set out to do so. However—"

"An accident," Jayne said. "Like Adele. Ironic, isn't it?"

Chapter 18

"How would Penner have known Al was Jayne's brother?" I asked. We were parked in the Port Dalhousie parking lot looking out at the lake.

"It's a small town. And, besides, if he had done that much digging into her history, he would have easily stumbled across her family details. It may not have meant anything to him until his daughter came home one day talking about her teacher. He put two and two together and..."

"And what? A plan is hatched? A killer is born?"

"Always so dramatic," Jeffers laughed. "No, but I imagine the name would have opened an old wound."

"You really think this is 'an eye for an eye'?"

"I think we need to talk to Penner."

"And Leland," I said. Jeffers cocked an eyebrow. "He's the one who brought up karma. He has just as much motive and maybe more opportunity given he's a student at the school. And he's the baby of the family. To have your mother taken from you in that way at that age … It would explain why he's so angry."

"And creepy."

"He is so creepy," I said through a giggle.

"All right, Penner and Leland."

Jeffers' phone vibrated. He looked at the screen. "Buddy from Edmonton," he said to me, then took the call.

"Shawn! How are you, man? Thanks for getting back to me. I've got you on speaker."

"Andre Jeffers! For crying out loud, I thought I was done with your ugly mug."

There was a back and forth of playful insults and a brief catching up before the boys got down to business.

"I'm afraid I couldn't find too much about the case you're looking for," Shawn said.

"I'll take whatever you've got," Jeffers replied.

"Looks like a cut-and-dried overdose. A bunch of university kids at a house party. 911 call came in about eleven on the night in question. Guy said there was a girl having a seizure. Ambulance was dispatched. Girl was dead when they got there."

"Girl's name?"

"Avril Leduc. Eighteen. Was visiting from out of town."

"What about the drugs?"

"Autopsy showed a mix of cocaine and alcohol. Not too much of it, but it was a bad combination and the girl was tiny according to this. Five-two, 103 pounds. Wouldn't have taken much."

"What do you mean a bad combination?" I asked.

"Shawn, this is Bella. She's working with me on this case."

"Oh, hey."

"Hi," I said. "Do you mean the drugs were laced with something?"

"No. Nothing like that. Just a bad mix of two strong substances in a little body. Heart couldn't take it."

"And I'm right in that there was no further investigation?"

"You are. This case was open and shut. Nothing suspicious. A typical party. Drinking and the odd sniff. Witnesses all said the girl was laughing and dancing, then she suddenly started to vomit and collapsed in seizure."

"And how long after she took the coke was that? Does it say?" Jeffers asked.

"Um..." There was a rustle of papers. "The autopsy report says it was likely the cocaine was in her system for about a half hour. Stomach contents were negligible, so that's another factor."

"And I'm sure the dancing didn't help," I said. "Since cocaine reduces the flow of oxygen to the heart, her heart would have already been working overtime."

"Yep."

I shook my head and closed my eyes. I didn't know what Avril looked like, but I pictured a young girl with some of Vince's features. Only softer. I imagined her excitement at getting to hang out with her older brother's university friends. How she probably wanted to impress them and appear more mature than she was. And how wanting so badly to fit into their world robbed her of ever reaching a similar place in her own.

"Does it say where the coke came from?" Jeffers asked. "I'm guessing someone at the party?"

More shuffling of papers. "Kid named Alan Macie."

Jeffers and I shot each other a look. I hadn't thought it possible for Macie's past to get any murkier.

"And there were never any charges laid?" I asked. "Possession or something?"

"Not according to this."

"But a girl died!"

"Looks to me like he paid a fine and that's it."

"Wow."

"Don't forget, this was twenty-some-odd years ago. Laws are different now."

"I get that, but still."

Jeffers and Shawn exchanged a bit more shop talk before signing off.

"We need to talk to Leduc," Jeffers said when he'd hung up.

"You got that right," I said.

Jeffers started the car and I could see him resist the urge to turn on the siren. I knew he was anxious for movement on this case, but even he could not justify a mad dash through the streets of the city just because he wanted to talk to someone. Even if this someone possibly held the key that would blow the investigation wide open.

I knew Leduc had a prep period three and would likely be in his office or the studio. We buzzed through to the secretary, identified ourselves, and were let into the school with no questions.

"Security sure is different from when I was in school," Jeffers said, commenting on the locked-door policy. "By the time Aden starts kindergarten it'll be retinal scans and thumbprints."

"You may not be too far off the mark," Principal Harvey said from the top of the stairs.

Jeffers finished his ascent and the two men shook hands.

"I heard you buzz through," Harvey said. "Figured I'd meet you. Does your being here mean there've been some developments?" He spoke in a whisper even though there was no one close enough to hear us.

"We do have some new information and—" Jeffers explained.

"New information?" Harvey asked. "Well, I hope I can be of help although I don't think I know any more than I've already told you." He made a move toward his office.

"We're actually here to talk to Mr. Leduc," Jeffers said.

The principal stopped in his tracks. "You think Vince had something to do with this?"

"There are just a few questions we're hoping he can help us with."

"I understand. Of course. But—"

"Is Vince in his office?" I asked. The question seemed to throw him off balance and he fumbled for an answer. "Mr. Harvey?"

"I saw him last in the cafeteria," he managed finally.

"Thank you," Jeffers said. "We can take it from here," he added when it looked as if the principal would join us.

"Yes," Harvey nodded. "Yes, of course."

Harvey followed us down the corridor with his gaze, becoming more and more of a Hitchcockian silhouette the further we got from him.

We met Leduc running up the steps just as we turned the corner into the stairwell.

"Bella!" he said, skidding to a halt. I could almost hear the screech of his sneakers. "And ... Dick Deadeye," he said, shifting his cellophane-wrapped sandwich and chocolate milk into one hand so he could shake Jeffers' hand with the other. "I'm so sorry, I've forgotten your name," he said with a smile.

"Detective Sergeant Jeffers."

"I must have missed that part last time," Vince said, still smiling.

"Is there somewhere we can talk?"

Vince shot a look to me.

"Jeffers is investigating Al's death," I explained.

"Is there somewhere private we can go?" Jeffers asked.

"I was heading outside to one of the picnic tables. Still a little chilly, but the sun is nice and every little bit of vitamin D helps." His smile never faltered. "If that's all right, Detective?"

"Lead the way."

"You don't mind if I eat?" Vince asked when we'd settled around one of the dozen or so picnic tables in the back courtyard of the school. There were a few students smoking at a table a few down from us, but neither Jeffers nor Leduc seemed to mind their presence. He tore open the wrapping without waiting for Jeffers' response.

"Mr. Leduc, I'd like to ask you a few questions about the night your sister died."

Vince coughed on his egg salad and spit it into a napkin. When he looked up, his smile had gone. I was surprised Jeffers had launched right in without any gentle lead up, but given that the meetings between the two men seemed to evolve into a virtual pissing contest, I really shouldn't have been.

"Detective … Jeffers, is it? I really don't see how my sister figures in here."

"Don't you? Your sister died of an overdose on drugs she got from Al Macie—"

"I'm well aware how my sister died—"

"You and Al had been best friends up to that point—"

"I don't know how digging up the past—"

"Your sister died at the hand of your best friend and he just walked away. Paid a piddly little fine and got on with his life. Meanwhile—"

"I don't like where this is headed, Detective! If you—"

"—you've been tracking Al for years. Plotting your revenge. Waiting for the right moment to exact retribution on the man who killed your sister by—"

"—think I had anything to do with Al's death, you are sorely mistaken! I made peace with what happened to Avril long ago. It was an accident. I had no reason to—"

"—killing him!"

"—kill him!"

The smokers stared as the crescendo reached its climax.

"Guys, would you mind heading inside?" I asked in my best teacher voice.

"But we—"

"Now, please!" Jeffers said, flashing his badge but never taking his eyes off Leduc. "Let's try this again," he said, when the students had gone. His voice calm, his manner relaxed.

Leduc held his gaze for another few seconds before inhaling deeply and easing his shoulders down. "Of course," he said.

"Can you tell me about the night Avril died?"

Jeffers had changed tactics completely. He asked the question this time around with sympathetic undertones and in a way that encouraged a civilized dialogue rather than a shouting match.

"Avril came to visit. She'd just graduated high school. I usually went home for the summer, but Al and I had gotten work doing Shakespeare in the park so she came out. We were very close. And she loved Al." He smiled at the memory. "She knew Al was gay but that didn't matter. She had her crush and that was that."

"What about the drugs?"

"Al had ... a guy. He usually had a pretty good stock of weed, but every now and then he'd get something else. For a party or something."

"Like cocaine."

"Mostly shrooms, or hash, or something like that, but yeah, sometimes coke."

"Did Al do a lot of drugs?"

"Not really. Like I said, we'd smoke a bit during the week, but the other stuff ... that was just usually for a special occasion or something."

"So, take me to the party."

"It was at this guy's place. A friend of the girl I was dating. We didn't really know the guy, but we wanted to show Avril a good time and we had nothing better to do."

"And Al brought cocaine to the party?"

Vince nodded. "It was just supposed to be for us. Avril wasn't even supposed to know about it, but she walked in on us and ... I don't know ... I guess she wanted to impress Al or something." He hesitated. "We fought."

"Who's 'we'?"

"Al and I. Avril and I. I didn't want her taking anything. She'd already had a couple of drinks. Al didn't see the harm in just a little and Avril wanted to try it."

"And what happened?"

"Isn't it obvious?" Jeffers waited. Vince went on. "Things got heated and I left."

"You left?" I asked. "The room? The party?"

"The party. I found my girlfriend and we left." My jaw dropped involuntarily. "Yes, Bella. The last time I saw Avril, we fought. I left my eighteen-year-old sister in the hands of my best friend and a half hour later she was dead."

Chapter 19

"He's lying. This is all part of his obsession. This fantasy he's created. And now he's made up this whole history! And for what purpose? To what end? Al is dead and he's still competing! Still trying to look like the better man by corrupting his memory. His reputation. Are you kidding me?" Glynn was fit to be tied. He paced the length of his living room. "What?" he said, looking at me and Jeffers. "You can't honestly tell me you believe him?"

"It all checks out," Jeffers said.

"Well, he must have—"

"Glynn—"

"You have no idea the lengths he'll go to. He—"

"Glynn!"

Glynn held Jeffers' gaze, defiant, then sank into the sofa with his head in his hands. "Why wouldn't he have told me?" he asked quietly.

"I don't know," I said gently. "Maybe he was ashamed. Maybe it was part of a private penance…"

"It doesn't make any sense. Al and I never kept secrets."

My mind flashed to Powell Avery and the dalliance he and Al had been involved in for years. Even if, as Powell had said, Al and Glynn had had an arrangement, now was certainly not the time to broach that topic.

"Okay," Glynn said, drying his eyes and shaking off the revelation, "so what does this mean? It gives Vince motive, right? Revenge. Premeditated. Why haven't you arrested him?"

"He has an alibi for the morning in question," Jeffers told Inspector Morris. We'd gone right to the police station following our visit to Glynn. "He says he was working out at White Oaks. I'm going to head over there later to check it out."

Morris gave a single nod. He was one of the most physically unimposing men I'd ever met, but the power in even his smallest gestures was palpable. He sat with his elbows propped up on his desk. His hands were clasped in front of him with his index fingers extended and resting against his lips. "You'll need access to their security footage?"

"Yes, sir."

Morris took a slip of paper from his desk, filled out several sections, signed it, and handed it to Jeffers. I didn't know what it said, but I guessed it was whatever was required to get the ball rolling on a search warrant of sorts.

"And Penner?"

Jeffers brought Morris up to speed on our interview with Jayne Evans. As was his way, Morris' expression never changed all the while Jeffers told the story nor when he had finished.

"I was waiting for the school day to finish before heading over. It's my next stop."

"How do you plan on speaking with them?"

"I'm sorry, sir?"

"Armin Penner and his children? You've said Armin Penner is a very controlling man. And, from what I gather, the younger son has followed suit with regard to his siblings. I doubt you will ever get the answers you need to further this investigation unless you find a way to speak with them individually and without each being influenced by another. So I ask again, how do you plan on speaking with them?"

"I…"

"I trust you'll figure it out, Detective. And quickly."

"Yes, sir."

Jeffers caught my eye and we rose to go.

"Detective Jeffers, we have two parties with very plausible reasons for wishing Al Macie harm. If Vincent Leduc's alibi is confirmed, we'll have one. You've got a busy evening ahead of you. I suggest you get moving."

"Thank you, sir."

We reached the door at the same time a manila envelope was slid underneath. This was followed by several smaller envelopes and, finally, a post card. Morris watched the parade of mail and rolled his eyes. Jeffers looked at Morris with a questioning eyebrow.

"Poor boy upset my chocolate milk once when he delivered the mail," Morris explained, coming out from behind his desk and collecting the small pile from the floor. "Been afraid to come in ever since. You're surprised, Ms. James?" he asked in response to the look of amazement I had directed at him before catching myself. "I am a human being with weaknesses like any other," he said, shuffling the envelopes, "My sweet tooth being the biggest."

"Of course, sir," I said, feeling the beginning heat of a blush on my cheeks.

He opened the door for us and returned to his desk without another word. We'd only managed a few steps before Morris appeared in his doorway, summoning us back in.

"You too, Ms. James," he called when I didn't immediately follow. "It's information Detective Jeffers will likely share with you anyway." From his tone I had no way of knowing whether he condoned the truth of this or had, perhaps, just resigned himself to the inevitability. Regardless, I hurried into the office before he had a chance to change his mind.

He handed Jeffers the manila envelope. "This just arrived."

"It's the forensics report on Macie," Jeffers said to me. "Seems to confirm everything we already surmised," he said, scanning the documents and nodding. Then he smiled and read, "'Tape liftings taken from the deceased show evidence of conspicuous foreign fibres on the victim's hands and under the fingernails. Greenish-blue viscose and polyester fibres were apparent. Fibres are not consistent with the victim's garments nor any material he may have had contact with in his home. Matching fibres were present in tape liftings taken from the school. Further analysis is pending.'"

He blurted out a few other findings but finished the report in silence.

"The killer was at the school. We knew that already," I said when Jeffers had finished.

"Yes, we did, Samuel. And now we know he was wearing aquamarine."

In the time it took us to leave Morris' office and get into Jeffers' car, there had been an explosion of aquamarine. It was the new black. And it was everywhere.

"There's another one," I said, pointing to a woman on the street with an aquamarine scarf wrapped around her neck. "That's five people since we left the station!"

"It's one of the trendy new colours," Jeffers said.

"This is more than a trend," I said. "This is … an epidemic." Jeffers laughed. "Look at his tie," I yelled, as we passed two men waiting at a crosswalk. "That's six, Jeffers. Six people and we've been in the car for what? Eight minutes? How am I just noticing it now?"

"Because now it's the colour of murder. It's how your mind works, Samuel. You can't help it. That's why you're here."

"Are you saying I can't help being drawn to the underworld?"

"An underworld with a pretty aquamarine sky," Jeffers said with a wink.

We pulled into the Penners' driveway. Corney was sanding paint off one of the window boxes. He smiled when he saw us.

"Detective," he said, coming off his ladder to shake Jeffers' hand. "If you're here to see Da, I'm afraid it's a wasted trip. He's gone off to see about some tractor parts. Don't expect him back for an hour or two."

"That's too bad," Jeffers said, feigning disappointment. As much as we needed to speak with Armin Penner, his absence solved the problem of getting time alone with both Leland and Ellie. "Since we're here, is your sister around?" he asked, as if the idea just occurred to him.

"Ellie's up in her room," Corney said then caught himself. "She's already spoken to you though."

"Yes, she's been most helpful. But sometimes shock can cause witnesses to leave out certain details. So we like to follow up with them after a period of time to review their statements. Give them a chance to fill in anything they might have missed." Corney was nodding, but I wasn't sure he was convinced. "Shouldn't take long," Jeffers added with a smile.

"El's only seventeen. Shouldn't my dad be here?"

"It's not necessary for something like this. She's not under arrest. We're just following up."

"I don't think Da would—"

"It's fine, Corney," Ellie said, appearing at an upstairs window. "Ms. James?"

"Hi, Ellie," I said.

"I didn't know you were police."

"I'm not. I'm just helping Detective Jeffers. Would you like to come down or should we—"

"Come up."

Corney let us in the front door and led the way up a carpeted staircase. Ellie stuck her head out of the door to her room and gave Corney a look. He retreated with an indignant sigh.

"I thought we were going to speak with Leland first," I whispered.

"Made more sense to start with the girl—she being the prime witness and all. Didn't want Corney asking more questions. I think it will be better this way. Armin doesn't seem to be as overprotective of his boys. Best to take full advantage of his absence."

"You can sit there, if you like," Ellie said when we'd entered her room. She indicated a window seat upholstered with cream and lilac flowers.

The room was large and very girly. Most of the decor was cream in base and accented by various shades of purple and pink. A dressing table sat to the left of the door as you came in; a stool with a cushion that matched the window seat was tucked neatly underneath. A chest of drawers stood against the far wall of the room. It boasted the very popular distressed finish that you'd find in a Pottery Barn catalogue, but I could see this was the real thing. This was a piece passed down through generations, as was the silver jewellery box with bevelled glass that sat atop it. There was also a white teddy bear holding a pink heart, and a framed photo of Adele.

There was something sad about the room. Almost like it never had a chance to become what it was supposed to have been. The room was modest in its simplicity, but the colours and decor indicated that, perhaps, there had been other plans for the space at one time. The walls were bare, but I could see faint outlines of where things had hung. Such embellishments would not be in keeping with the current vocation, I guessed.

I imagined Adele and Ellie picking out furniture and fabrics, knick-knacks and decorations; Ellie wanting a room for a princess and Adele wanting to give that to her; the excitement that would have gone into making it absolutely perfect. I smiled as I remembered doing something similar with my own mother. It wasn't princesses, it was panda bears. And it was wonderful.

Ellie sat on the edge of a double bed that looked hastily made for our benefit. I moved to the window seat. Jeffers stood by the dressing table.

"You're sure you're comfortable talking to us without your father here?" Jeffers asked. He was covering his bases. There is no law stating that a minor needs to have a parent present when speaking with police, but they do need to be given the choice.

Ellie nodded.

"I know it was a terrible shock for you to have discovered Mr. Macie the way you did." Ellie nodded again.

"How are you doing now?"

She shrugged. "Sometimes I have a hard time sleeping. I see him when I close my eyes."

"Of course," Jeffers said. "That's completely natural. But it will get better. You know we have a program downtown if you ever want to talk to someone."

"I'm okay."

"Okay," Jeffers said with a kind smile. "Ellie, we often like to follow up with witnesses after something like this. We find that sometimes the shock of what was seen can cause someone to forget certain details and that, often, these things can be recalled over time. Do you mind if we go over what you remember from that morning?"

"Sure."

"Good." Jeffers took out his notebook and flipped through the pages. "Now, Ellie, you said you came to the school early to study for a test…"

Ellie's eyes looked to me.

"You were there to see Mr. Macie, weren't you?" I asked. Her eyes lowered. "It's all right, Ellie. You can tell us. You're not in any trouble."

"I didn't mean to lie," she said. "My dad was there and if he knew…"

"He's not here now," Jeffers said gently. "Why don't you tell us what happened."

Ellie got up and closed her bedroom door, then looked to the window to make sure it was closed. She didn't speak again until she was back on the bed.

"I don't know what Ms. James has told you," she said. Her eyes were averted but she was clearly speaking to Jeffers.

"I know you were receiving some private coaching from Mr. Macie," Jeffers said.

He did not explain that he also knew her father disapproved and had threatened Al if he didn't end the arrangement. He was likely waiting to see if she'd offer this information on her own. Even if it meant implicating him in Macie's death. He didn't have to wait long.

Chapter 20

Ellie explained how she came to take Al Macie's course off the record and how that had led to the private sessions. She included her father's objections and her brother's tattling and finally got to the meeting that occurred between Armin and Macie the day before he died.

"My father was furious when he found out I hadn't dropped the class like I'd promised," she said.

"And how did he find out?" I asked.

"Mr. Macie and I always met in the morning. One or two times a week. Before classes started. My brother came to school a little earlier than usual one day and…"

"Saw you?"

"The door was open and he just happened by. He wasn't spying on me or anything. It wasn't like that."

I didn't believe that for a second.

"Did he interrupt the session?" Jeffers asked.

"No. But he waited for me at my locker and told me he'd seen us. Said I'd brought shame to our family. That I'd acted against the teachings of the church. Said he was going to tell Da. I begged him not to. I told him I'd end it. I promised, but…" She shook her head. "My father came to the school during lunch. He confronted Mr. Macie. I'd never seen him so angry."

"You were there?" I asked.

"Mr. Macie had already gone against my father's wishes by continuing to coach me in secret. I knew Leland was going to tell. And I knew it would only be a matter of time before my father flipped out. But I didn't think it would be so soon. I went to his office to warn him."

"You heard their conversation?" Jeffers asked.

"Not all of it. When I got there, Mr. Macie was trying to reason with my dad, but he wasn't having any of it. He kept going on about sin, and deceit, and about how what Mr. Macie was doing was inappropriate and that he was going to tell Mr. Harvey if he didn't stop seeing me."

"What did Mr. Macie say to that?"

"Nothing."

"What do you mean 'nothing'?" I asked.

"I expected him to fight for me. He was always saying how talented I was. How I had something special. How I should never give up on my dream. That I should stand by what I believe in and what I want and not to let anything stand in my way." Jeffers and I shared a look. "But he didn't say any of that. He just gave in. Assured my father there would be no more coaching and that I would no longer be permitted to take his class." There was a fire behind her eyes.

"What happened then?" Jeffers asked.

"My dad left."

"And you?"

"I was so hurt and angry, you know? I couldn't believe Mr. Macie had just given up like that. I mean, who cares if my dad told Mr. Harvey?"

Ellie clearly had no idea what implications came with an accusation of inappropriate behaviour and neither Jeffers nor I jumped to fill her in.

"Did you speak with Mr. Macie?" I asked.

She nodded. "I told him I'd overheard and I begged him to change his mind. He just kept telling me how sorry he was but there was nothing more he could do. But it didn't make any sense. I said he was…"

"It's okay, Ellie, go on," I urged.

"I'm afraid I said some not very nice things. I was so upset. I didn't mean them, really. I was so … I don't know … I felt like I'd lost everything that mattered. Again."

"Do you mean your mom?" I asked, carefully.

Ellie nodded, her eyes lowered. Jeffers raised his index finger to me in an appeal to wait before broaching the subject of Adele any further.

"Ellie, what happened the next morning? You went to the school early. You didn't have a coaching session and you weren't studying for a test, so why?" Jeffers asked.

"I wanted to apologize for the awful things I'd said. And I figured out a way Mr. Macie could keep coaching me without anybody finding out."

"What do you mean?"

"Leland always comes home for lunch. Always. He has chores he *has* to do."

"So that's why you told Mr. Leduc your sessions have to be during lunch?" I asked.

"There was always a risk of Leland being at the school in the morning but never at lunch. I thought Mr. Macie would be thrilled that we could keep working together. At least up to my audition. I mean, I knew I'd have to give up the class but as long as I could keep moving forward with the audition … I wasn't giving up. Just like Mr. Macie told me. I thought he'd be proud of me. I thought he'd be happy. But he just kept repeating everything he had said the day before. He wouldn't even give it a chance."

"Wait a minute. You spoke with Mr. Macie that morning? He was alive?" Jeffers asked.

"Y-es."

"Ellie, why didn't you say something before?" I asked, trying to keep the urgency in my voice from scaring her off.

"If my dad found out I went to see him, I..."

Jeffers brought his hands to his face and let out a long exhale. "Okay," he said. "It's okay." The first was to himself. The second was to the imaginary powers that be. There'd been a shift in the feel of the room. The energy swirling, picking up speed.

"Ellie, when was this? What time, exactly?" He asked, fighting to keep his voice calm.

"Exactly? I don't know *exactly*. I got there around six. It's only a short walk to the school."

Jeffers nodded and took out his notebook.

"And how long were you with Macie? Mr. Macie?"

"Not long. It was like he didn't want to talk to me at all. He wouldn't even let me in the office."

"Five minutes? Ten?"

"I'm ... not ... sure ..."

"Think!"

"Jeffers," I warned. "It's fine, Ellie. Whatever you can remember."

"Maybe ten? If that."

"Great," I said, smiling. Jeffers scribbled.

"Ellie," he said, still writing. "I need you to think very carefully now." She nodded. "Did you see anyone else at the school?"

"No."

"Anyone at all? This is very important." She shook her head. "Damn."

"Ellie, can I ask how you knew Mr. Macie would be at the school that early?" I asked.

"He told me. Well, not just me, the class."

"Did Mr. Macie often share personal details like that?"

"Yeah. We had a thing called a weekly check-in where we had a chance to talk about how we were feeling or if anything was bothering us or whatever."

"I see," I said, thinking how I would have absolutely hated if it had been in practice when I was in school. "And how did you get in?" Given that security was tight during regular hours, I could only imagine getting into the school at that time of the morning would require an enchanted key and a magic spell.

"The janitor's door," Ellie said, matter-of-factly. "The janitors get there super early and they always leave it open."

I glanced at Jeffers, who made a note.

"You told your father you were meeting a friend to study for a test, but isn't six kind of early? He didn't find that odd?"

"Ms. James, we all have chores in the morning. Mine is to make breakfast and do the washing up. I slipped out early, when they were all outside. I knew Mr. Macie would be at the school and I wanted to be sure to talk with him as soon as possible. After he told me there was no way he could continue coaching me, I left. I came home. I did the breakfast and the dishes. No one even knew I'd been gone."

"But…"

"I was so upset and just wanted to be alone. So I told my dad I was meeting a friend to study for a test and I went back to the school early."

"And that's when you found Mr. Macie's body?" Jeffers asked.

Ellie nodded.

"Can you remind me," Jeffers said, flipping through his notes, "did you just happen to walk by the studio? Or were you heading there for a specific reason…?"

"Some of my stuff was there."

"And what time was this?" Jeffers asked.

"I don't know. We usually finish breakfast around seven, so it must have been a little after that."

The timeline checked out with what we already knew.

Jeffers got up from where he was leaning against the dressing table and began to pace. "You're sure, you're absolutely positive you didn't see anyone else at the school?"

"I—"

"What's going on?" a voice said from the doorway. Leland stood there watching us. Jeffers and I had been so focused on Ellie, neither one of us had heard him open the door.

"It's all right, Lee," Ellie said. "They just had a few more questions."

"Should you be talking to her without Da here?" he asked Jeffers.

"I can assure you, we're all well within our rights." Jeffers said. "As a matter of fact, we'd love to have a word with you too, if you have a moment."

"I got nothing to say."

"You may think you don't know anything that will help, but you might be surprised."

Leland looked to Ellie. She met his gaze and held it, almost defiantly, before looking away.

"I'll be in the barn," he said and left the room.

"I'm sorry about him," Ellie said. "He's very … protective. Ever since our mother died."

"Is this her?" I asked, indicating the photo on the dresser. Ellie nodded. "She's beautiful. You look just like her."

She smiled. "I have my dad's nose though."

"The best features of both."

"Ellie, where did you say Leland was that morning?"

"Where he always is. In the orchard."

Jeffers muttered under his breath and scribbled something in his book.

"Actually, no," Ellie said. "Maybe he was in the barn. Or the cellar. I don't know. I just remembered Corney complaining at breakfast about having to do all the work himself because Lee took off somewhere."

Chapter 21

"Where did you go on the morning Mr. Macie was killed?" Jeffers asked, entering the barn where Leland was waiting, as promised. There was no acknowledgment from the teen, and Jeffers repeated his question, raising his voice to be heard over the sound of scraping metal.

Leland balanced on a wobbly stool in front of an old wooden table that served as a workbench. A block of wood was secured to the table by a couple of clamps and a sharpening stone sat on the block, kept in place by a fence of nails. Pruners, shears, shovels, and blades of various kinds sat in neat little rows like well-behaved children with their hands in the air and "pick me" on their faces. He looked up at us through safety goggles. "I heard you the first time," he said, making no move to stop what he was doing.

Jeffers bristled at the affront. I put my hand gently on his arm and gave a warning look to be patient. Although I shook my head at the audacity of this fifteen-year-old boy, I knew exactly what Leland was doing. The game he was playing. The power he thought he had. I knew because I had been the same at his age. Putting on a tough exterior. Acting the bully or adopting attitude because of the sense of control it gave. I hadn't been able to control my grief or circumstances, so I got power in other ways. I looked at

Leland's strong arms and broad shoulders hunched over the sharpening stone. There was a grimace on his face and a tightness in his jaw, and although his eyes were obscured by the goggles, I was sure they were darkened by the shadow of pain. For all his brawn and bravado, Leland was just a little boy who'd lost his mother.

He passed the blade over the stone one more time before putting it alongside its kin, then lifted the goggles onto his head and took a rag from his back pocket. He looked at us while he wiped his hands. I stared at the rag. It was grimy from use, but there was no mistaking the colour.

My eyes did a quick scan of the barn's interior and came to rest on a package of identical, clean rags tucked away on a shelf. The blue was so vibrant against the weathered brown of the barn's walls it made me wonder how my eye had not been immediately drawn there when we'd entered.

"I was in the orchard."

"Ellie said you weren't," Jeffers said. "She told us your brother had complained about having to do all the chores himself."

"Her name is Elsbeth," he said gruffly. "And Corney complains about everything."

I wondered if there was something behind the fact that it was only Ellie's name he seemed to have a problem with shortening.

"So where were you?" Jeffers asked again.

"We got a lot of chores here that need doing. I could've been on a run, or down in the cellar…"

"Which one is it?"

"I don't … remember. What's the big deal?"

"The big deal," Jeffers started, "is that a man is dead."

Leland crossed his arms over his barrel chest and rolled his eyes.

"Leland," I said.

"Who are *you* anyway? You're at the school, you're here, at the store. It's like I can't get away from you."

I ignored the question. "You told your father your sister was taking Mr. Macie's class and was meeting him privately for coaching. Why did it bother you so much?"

"Because it's not right."

"Why?

"Because," he said a little louder. Jeffers took a casual step toward him. "It's not respectable," he said a little more calmly. "It goes against the doctrine. The things they do in that class. And meeting a man alone. It's not proper. It's not what we're taught. It's sinful."

It sounded to me like Leland was simply restating what he'd heard his father say with very little understanding as to why he'd said it.

"She's always doing stuff like that," he continued, a hint of petulance colouring his words.

"Like what?" Jeffers asked.

"Stuff. Going places. Reading ... books. Corney too! Always listening to music and sneaking off to the movies. They think no one knows. But we know. Me and Da. And when Da's too busy to take care of things, it's up to me." He said the last proudly.

"Did you take care of Mr. Macie?"

"I ... what?"

"Where were you on the morning Mr. Macie was killed?"

"I told you. I was—"

"You weren't in the orchard. And I don't think you were in the cellar, or on a run, or out here in the barn."

"I..."

"Your sister went to see Mr. Macie that morning around six. Did you know that?"

Leland looked at Jeffers. For a fraction of a second he was a scared little boy caught in a lie and terrified about what might happen. But only for a fraction of a second.

"Did you follow her to school?"

"What if I did?"

"What happened when you got there?"

Leland held Jeffers' gaze and for a few moments neither of them spoke.

"I don't want to talk to you anymore," Leland said finally.

Jeffers inhaled deeply and exhaled a retreat. He could not force Leland to say anything further without charging him with something, and he knew he still didn't have enough grounds to do that. It was my turn to try something.

"Do you remember what you said to me at the store? About karma?"

Leland shrugged.

"You said Mr. Macie got what he deserved."

"So?"

"That's a pretty strong statement."

Again with a shrug.

"You think his death is what he deserved because of Ellie—"

"Elsbeth!"

"Or your mother?"

Leland came off the stool toward me with an agility contrary to his build. Jeffers was between us in seconds and rested a hand against Leland's chest. It brought to mind David and Goliath as Jeffers barely came to the boy's shoulders and I couldn't help but repress a giggle.

"Calm down, son," Jeffers said.

"I'm not your 'son,'" Leland said, looking down at Jeffers, challenging him with his eyes.

"No, but you're mine, and I'll advise you to show some respect," Armin Penner said from where he stood in the entrance to the barn, backlit by the sun. I couldn't see the expression on his face, but the tone of his voice indicated he was far from pleased with finding us there. In spite of the warning he'd given to his son.

"Yes, sir," Leland said and moved back to the stool, throwing the rag into a nearby trash bin.

"Perhaps you'd like to tell me what's got my boy so upset," Armin said, looking first to Jeffers then to me.

"We'd like to know where he was the morning Al Macie was killed," Jeffers explained.

"He was here," Armin said.

"We're not so sure about that."

Armin looked to Leland who looked away.

"Son?"

"I saw Elsbeth sneak out so I followed her," Leland said begrudgingly then added more forcefully, "I didn't kill anybody."

"Did you know she was going to the school?" Armin asked.

"I figured. You guys were screaming about it all night. I knew she'd probably try something."

Armin's jaw tightened. He looked slightly embarrassed and avoided meeting our eyes.

"What happened when you got there?" Jeffers asked.

Leland hesitated. "I didn't hear all that good, but Elsbeth tried to get Mr. Macie to keep coaching her and he said he couldn't. She left all upset."

"Was she alone?"

"What?"

I knew why Jeffers was asking. Ellie, on her own, wouldn't have been able to overpower Macie, but with some help...

Jeffers repeated the question. Leland nodded.

"Leland, did you see anyone else at the school? Anyone at all?"

Leland gave the briefest of glances toward his father before lowering his eyes and shaking his head.

"Detective, I think that'll be all for today," Armin said.

"We'd—"

"If you have anything further to discuss with me or my children, I'm sure we can find a more suitable time. At present, there is work to be done that cannot wait."

He looked to Leland, who made a swift exit from the barn. Then he looked to Jeffers, who followed. I too made my way to the door, clumsily knocking over the trash bin as I did so.

"It's definitely them," Jeffers said, starting up the car. "Did you see the way Leland looked at his father when I asked if he'd seen anyone else at the school? They're covering!"

"Armin seemed genuinely surprised to find out Leland had been at the school that morning."

"Is that how it looked to you? It's an act, Bella! You should be able to see that better than anyone! One of them killed Macie and the other one knows it. Maybe even helped stage the suicide. Hell, maybe Ellie's involved too. A real family affair! I am close, Bella, I am close and I will prove it."

I was feeling the sting from Jeffers' comment but shrugged it off. I had been present during one of these mood swings before. I knew he was feeling the pressure and that it wasn't personal.

"Maybe this will help," I said, laying Leland's dirty rag on Jeffers' lap when we'd gotten far enough away from the house.

"How did—"

"It must have fallen into my purse when I was tidying up the stuff I knocked over," I said innocently.

"Detective Samuel!"

"Oh, give me a break, it's all legal. Once something is in the garbage it's anyone's property. See, I did learn a few useful things on the show."

"I wasn't scolding. That was my impressed voice."

"Well, then, thank you very much," I said, channelling my best Elvis. Jeffers rolled his eyes.

"I'll get it to the lab. It's a stretch, but there's a chance fibres from a rag like this could have gotten onto the attacker's clothing and from there could have been easily transferred to Macie. This is good. This is … something," Jeffers said, then slammed his hand against the steering wheel in frustration. "Damn, why is this so hard?"

We drove in silence. Jeffers had gone from sure to doubtful in a matter of seconds.

"Do you think we might be looking in the wrong places?" I asked after a while. "We've been so focused on the Penners and Vince—"

"Because the Penners and Vince have motives!"

"Maybe someone else does too?"

"You're not helping."

Jeffers drove on, pouting.

"Why? Why do you think that?" he finally asked.

"I don't know," I said. "It just seems that we should have found something definitive by now."

"You think Macie messed with a bunch of other guys' sisters and wives and they're all seeking revenge at the same time?"

"Jeffers, that's not what I—"

"Or maybe he was having an affair with one of the Smurfs, thus the aquamarine!"

"Now you're just being childish."

This earned me an almost imperceptible snarl but not another word until we pulled into my driveway.

"I'm sorry," he said. I'm just..."

"I know."

"I'm going to drop this rag at the lab then I'm going to White Oaks to check out Vince's alibi," Jeffers said. "Hopefully one of those trips will pay off."

"Hopefully," I echoed, getting out of the car.

"I'll call you," he said, then honked a goodbye and drove off.

Moustache was on the sofa, sandwiched between two throw cushions, with all four feet in the air. He heard me come in and struggled to right himself. One of the cushions fell to the floor followed by the dog, who gave a quick shake before bounding over to me. With my hands ruffling either side of his head, I brought my forehead to meet his and kissed the bridge of his nose. He gave a happy snort then wriggled free and ran to the back door. My phone rang.

"Hey, you," I said to Paul as I let Moustache out into the yard.

"Hi. I'm just at the store. I don't know what you have planned for supper, but I thought I'd check in to see if you need anything."

I screamed silently. It was my night to cook and I'd completely forgotten.

"Bells?"

"Um…"

"Did you forget?"

"No-o," I lied, frantically opening cupboards.

"It's okay," he said, on to me and laughing. "I'm right here. I can pick up anything. What do you have a taste for?"

I knew he'd end up cooking, which wasn't fair given that I'd had the day off, technically, and he'd spent his in and out of procedures. I continued to rummage, my eyes finally resting on a box tucked away on a shelf.

"I've got everything under control," I said.

"You're sure?"

"It'll be ready in … twenty minutes," I said, checking the directions on the box. "You, my dear, are in for a treat."

"I've tried it with honey garlic, but I think the hot Italian works better," I said, as we walked off our supper. Moustache ran ahead, as far as his leash would allow.

"Whatever you used was great."

"I can't believe you've never had macaroni and cheese with sausage before. Not even with hot dogs?"

"Nope."

"Wow. I thought that was a staple in every home."

"My mother only cooked from scratch, even though we begged her to buy the boxed stuff. She'd slave over the stove, using the best cheeses and fancy shaped pasta. It was delicious, but it wasn't the same. Of course, I'd never tell her that. Not to this day. Now Dan Manure's mom, she knew how to rock a box of mac and cheese. No hot dogs though. She used to sprinkle broken Doritos on top."

"What about Laura?" I asked tentatively.

Paul hesitated and I could tell he was holding his breath. Or maybe it had just caught in his throat.

"She was a vegetarian," he said finally. "Used to douse hers in ketchup. But we didn't have it very often."

"I'm sorry. I shouldn't have asked."

"No, it's … it's fine."

"She was a huge part of your life," I said. "You don't have to hide that from me."

The words came out of my mouth dripping in hypocrisy. I had spent practically my whole life in hiding. With the exception of Natalie, there was no one who had been privy to my inner clockwork. Jeffers had seen glimpses and so had Paul, but I was still very careful about exposing too much. It was a practice I knew I had to break and I was working on it. Slowly.

He squeezed my hand but didn't say anything else. We stopped while Moustache sniffed a bush and tried to decide which leg to lift against it.

"Are dogs left- or right-pawed? Like people?" I asked.

"Male dogs tend to be left-pawed and females, right."

"Really?"

"It's not always the case, but…"

"How can you tell?"

"Put a piece of tape on the dog's nose. See which paw he uses to try and get it off."

"Shut up," I said through a giggle.

"It's true! There's a lot of research that has gone into paw preference. There are differences in emotional patterns and behavioural characteristics, trainability, levels of aggression … It's sometimes what determines whether a dog is suited for military service or a career as a therapy dog. Right and left brain, you know. Same as us."

"Huh."

We started walking again.

"You're going to do it, aren't you?" he said.

"What?"

"Put tape on Moustache's nose."

"I ... no!" I said with as much indignation as I could muster. "Well ... maybe ... no!" I was totally going to.

He laughed and squeezed my hand again.

"So remind me again who's having the affair with a Smurf," he said.

I had not gone into too much detail with Paul, but I had hinted at some of the day's highlights, including Jeffers' not-so-clever punchline.

"Oh god," I said, rolling my eyes. Then I stopped. "Oh god!"

"You okay?"

"Can you take this?" I asked, handing over Moustache's leash. I pulled out my phone and dialed Jeffers. Paul and Moustache walked ahead.

"What if Macie's relationship with Powell wasn't as casual as Powell made it out to be?" I said when Jeffers answered.

"Hang on," he said and covered the receiver. There was a muffled conversation, then Jeffers came back on the line. "Sorry, what?" I repeated my theory. "You think Macie was in love with Powell?"

"Probably the other way around," I said, thinking back to how Powell had referred to their relationship as "dating" when it really wasn't. Maybe he had wanted it to be. "While I think it's likely that Glynn and Al had an understanding of sorts, I don't think there was ever a question of Al leaving Glynn."

"Which is exactly the kind of thing lovers fight about."

"And we know how this particular fight ended."

Chapter 22

Powell Avery was standing in a corner of the rehearsal room, deep in conversation with Adam, when I arrived at the theatre the following morning. His hands were resting casually on his hips and he nodded as Adam spoke. After a few moments, they both laughed. Powell clapped Adam on the back and moved to put his things down in another part of the room. Adam caught my eye and slunk over.

"Your master plan seems to be coming along," I said.

"Not as well as I would like, but I'm working on it," he said with a wink.

"So you still haven't asked him out?"

"Not exactly."

"What does that mean?"

"Well, we went out the other night. But before you get excited, it wasn't a date. We were at that talk the *Uncle Vanya* director was giving about Russian manners and etiquette—"

"I thought that was just for the cast."

"No. It was open to the company."

"And *you're* interested in Russian manners and etiquette?"

Adam dramatically brought a hand to his chest and scoffed in great offence. "I'll have you know—"

"You heard Powell was going, didn't you?"

"Yep," he said, dropping the act. "Anyway, when it was over we went for a drink. No big deal."

"That's kind of a big deal! You've wanted to go out with him for weeks."

"We were in a group. But we sat next to each other, so…"

"You seemed to be getting along just now, so you obviously didn't put him off with your manners, Russian or otherwise."

"He is a tough nut to crack," he said, looking at Powell wistfully. "Pun intended. But I've met harder challenges face on. Pun intended there too."

I groaned. Adam shrugged proudly at his own cleverness. Blue as it was.

"He's a good guy, right?" I asked.

"What do you mean?"

"I just … wouldn't want you to get hurt."

"Sweetie, don't rain on my parade."

"I'm not raining!"

"You're a doll to care, but I'm a big boy and I can take care of myself."

My mind flashed to Al Macie, who probably thought the same thing.

The assistant stage manager, Courtney, approached. She had worked at the Festival for a number of years but had never been able to move to the helm of her own show. This was a chip that weighed heavily on her shoulder, osmosed into her pores, and oozed out on the backs of every word she spoke. "Adam, I need you to show me exactly how you want your briefcase to be set on the train."

"What you've been doing is fine."

After a sigh that simply dripped in disdain, she managed, "Can you just…"

Adam took a deep breath and flashed me the briefest of eye rolls. "Sure," he said and moved off in the direction of the props table.

Courtney followed, dragging her heels and shaking her head at the menial tasks that made up her life's work. I sidled up to Powell.

"Hey, do you have a sec?"

"Hi. What's up?" I nodded toward the hallway. "Everything okay?" he asked, following me out of the room.

"Yeah. I hope so. I mean ... yes. I just have a couple of—" I cut myself off. My breath was catching in my throat and I thought I might hyperventilate.

"Bella?"

"I'm fine," I said then blurted, "Were you in love with Al? Macie? Were you in love with Al Macie?"

Powell ran his fingers through his hair and gave one of those laughs that people give when they find something incredulous.

"Were you?" I repeated.

"What is this about?"

"The police—"

"Oh my god," Powell said, drawing me in deep into a corner. "Are you kidding me? Do they think I had something to do with Al's death?"

"Powell—"

"Do *you*? Jesus, how do the police even know about me and Al?"

"The police don't. Just one detective. It came out when we were looking into Al's sister. I'm sorry."

"I don't believe this."

Calmly I said, "Powell, we know Al's death was an accident. Sometimes things can get heated between lovers, especially when one feels more deeply about the relationship and—"

"And what? I killed Al because he wasn't in love with me?"

"It happens."

"It didn't!"

"So what did?"

"Bella!" His eyes pleaded with mine for a moment then shifted their gaze to the ceiling as his head leaned against the wall behind him. "What Al and I felt for each other, I don't expect you to understand. But there was never any chance of it being more than what it was."

"Because of Glynn?"

"Because of me!" He said, his voice rising. "Because of Al! Because that's not what we were to each other. That's not what we wanted from each other! That's why it worked!" He took a breath and when he spoke again, it was quiet and steady. "Did I love Al? Maybe I did. Was I upset when he suggested we call things off for a while? Yes. Did I kill him? God, Bella, I'm not even going to dignify that with a response."

He moved toward the door to the rehearsal hall.

"Why did he end things?"

He stretched out his arms in an exasperated "I don't know." "He got weird when we were away together the last time. Said we should cool things. Even cut the weekend short. I didn't argue. And, before you ask, I never saw him again."

"What did he mean by 'weird'?" Jeffers asked when I called him later during a rehearsal break.

"He didn't elaborate. Maybe he just started to feel guilty about cheating on Glynn."

"Or maybe something spooked him."

"Maybe."

"Can you find out where they were?"

"What?"

"You said they'd go away for the weekend? Where did they go?"

"I don't know. He didn't say."

"Can you find out?"

I hesitated.

"Are you still there?"

"Yeah," I said. "I can't, Jeffers."

"Why not?"

"I just ... I don't want to push it."

"It's just a question."

"It's not. It's ... Jeffers, I work with Powell. Very closely. There's a trust that actors build together. Maybe because you're vulnerable so often or maybe because figuring out the journey means trying new things and failing spectacularly. I don't know. But there's safety. You tell the story together. There's a trust. And I jeopardized that today."

Powell had been professional since our chat and we'd even had a great discussion with the director about a moment near the end of the show where Sally tells Cliff that she's ended her pregnancy and that he should return to America without her. But there was no banter or regular teasing. No casual conversation or friendly touches. No one else would have noticed. But I did.

"Well, since the damage is already done..." Jeffers said, trying to add some lightness to the situation. When I didn't respond he added, "Okay, I'm sorry. I get that this is tough, but he could very well hold key information." I stayed silent. "Samuel, we are at a dead end. Maybe it's the

Penners and maybe it's Vince. Or, like you said, maybe it's someone else. We have nothing solid."

"What happened at White Oaks? Vince's alibi?"

"According to the computer login, he arrived at the club as soon as it opened at five thirty and left at seven. There's video of him coming and going and walking into the weight room, but once he's in there…"

"I don't imagine there's coverage everywhere. My god, there's got to be some privacy. Let people sweat in peace."

"No, that's not it. The cameras show a pretty clear view of the weight room at all times. We see Leduc go in, but then nothing. He vanishes."

"What?"

"I have some guys going over the frames at an excruciatingly slow speed right now and I'm on my way back there to walk his route. Get a physical lay of the land. So you see, nothing solid. And we're almost out of time! You need to talk to Powell!"

"Jeffers—"

"Or I'm going to have to bring him in."

I shifted the weight of the world from one shoulder to the other and returned to the rehearsal hall. Powell and all his stuff were gone.

"Evidently, he said he wasn't feeling well and asked if he could be excused from the rest of the call. He was only scheduled for one more scene and he really didn't have much to do in it, so his absence really didn't put anyone out."

We were at Paul's place and had just finished supper. A rumble of thunder sounded outside and he got up, made sure the cat door was unlocked, and pulled a can of cat food out of a kitchen cupboard.

"You think that's true?" he asked.

"He seemed fine to me. My instincts are telling me he's not involved, but why would he run?"

"Being asked if you killed the person you loved can have all kinds of effects. None of them good," he said, opening the can and spooning the food into a small bowl.

There was another round of thunder and the beginning of rain. Paul set the bowl on the floor, took a quick peek out the back window, and returned to the living room. To me. He sat with his back against the arm of the sofa and put his feet in my lap.

"Did they ask you that? When Laura…"

"Isn't that what good police officers are supposed to do?"

"I'm sorry. That must have been awful."

"Give him some time," he said, "If he's not involved, he'll understand you were just doing your job. And if he is…"

"But it's not my job, is it? Not really."

He smiled and worked his feet and legs to move me closer to him. The rain was falling steadily now. The thunder was more frequent and it seemed as if the wind had picked up. I brought my lips to his and he wrapped his arms around me. My hands reached up to caress the back of his head and brushed against something cold and wet.

Brimstone was sitting on the top of the sofa, soaked through, and not happy about it.

"Don't move," Paul whispered.

"How did he get here? I didn't hear a thing!"

"Shh."

We sat in still silence as Brimstone glared, clearly holding us responsible for the rain that forced him inside and for the indignity of his current appearance. Usually majestic and fierce looking, the storm had flattened his coat to his frame revealing a skinny truth. I pursed my lips to contain a threatening giggle. Paul caught my eye and put a warning finger to his lips.

The cat was steadfast in his disdain and blame and positively oozed contempt for the both of us. The urge to giggle quickly vanished and was replaced by a fervent wish for one of the protective rubber suits the vet techs had been wearing during his recent visit to the clinic. I didn't see how this could possibly end with me and Paul coming out of it unscathed, let alone alive. I closed my eyes and prayed for a quick death.

What we got instead was a shower of mud and wet as Brimstone shook himself with all his might. We remained still and dripping while he stalked back and forth along the sofa's back, and when he finally, stealthily, jumped to the floor and began to walk away, I involuntarily released a whimper that earned me a parting hiss.

Paul pulled me close and we laughed gratefully, albeit quietly, sure we had just survived a near miss of the reaper's scythe. I lay in Paul's arms, listening to the tinkle of Brimstone's tags against his dish. Thinking of Laura. Thinking of Paul and Laura. Thinking of how to repair things with Powell; of Jeffers and Glynn and Vince and the Penners. Of Al Macie. And of the answers that were out there, taunting us, eluding us, waiting for us.

Chapter 23

"Where have you been?" Jeffers asked, exiting his car that was sitting in my driveway.

"I was over at—how long have you been here?"

Through the passenger window, I could see Jeffers' front seat was littered with empty remnants of takeout coffee and snacks.

"It doesn't matter. I gotta show you something."

Moustache danced circles on our arrival, jumping back and forth from me to Jeffers, his whole body wiggling and his mouth open in excitement. Jeffers passed the sniff test and was allowed entry into the kitchen. I was detained under an umbrella of suspicion. His nose worked up one of my pant legs and down the other without getting any satisfaction. It was like Brimstone had left just enough of a trace to drive the dog crazy but not provide any definitive answers.

"Do you have anything to eat?" Jeffers asked. I could hear him rummaging through the fridge.

"Are you kidding me?" I said, wrenching free from Moustache's probing snout and ushering him to the back door. "Your car looks like you've been in a burger-tasting competition. How are you hungry?"

"That's not all from today."

As long as I'd known Jeffers, he'd always kept his car immaculate. A speck of dirt would think twice before falling off a shoe and onto the floor mat.

"Lately a drive is the only thing that will quiet the baby. I've been taking him out in the night so Aria can sleep."

He pulled a plastic container from the fridge, smelled its contents, and made a face.

"It's curry," I said.

"Doesn't smell like curry. It smells like … I don't know what. Not curry. Are those…"

"Raisins."

"In curry?"

"Give me that," I said, taking the container and replacing the lid. It was my lunch for the following day. "Here," I said, tossing Jeffers a loaf of bread and some fixings.

He set about making a sandwich while I put the kettle on. Moustache scratched furiously at the back door as if every raindrop that fell onto his fur was a flaming poison arrow. He darted into the house, tolerated a once-over with a towel, and reattached his nose to my pants. I pulled a rawhide strip out of the cupboard and held it out for him. Normally, he would have snatched it and run out of the room to chew it in privacy, but today he was hell-bent on decoding whatever message Brimstone had left. It seemed the cat had woven quite a mystery. An amazing feat given that I'd had virtually no contact with the fiend. But I supposed the reach of evil could extend far beyond what one could imagine. I threw the rawhide, hoping a little play might entice Moustache away from me. He didn't budge.

"What did you want to show me?"

"It would seem," Jeffers said, holding his sandwich in one hand and operating his laptop with the other, "that our dear Mr. Leduc was not where he claimed to be on the morning of the murder."

"What? I thought the surveillance video showed him at White Oaks?"

"It does. It shows him arriving at five thirty and walking into the weight room, and it shows him exiting out a back door at approximately five forty-five."

Jeffers played the video and there, clear as day, was Vincent Leduc talking briefly with a man using a leg press before heading toward the towel rack in the back. Then I lost him.

"There," Jeffers said, pointing at the screen. I could barely make him out through the grid of machines and the rising and falling of arms and legs, not to mention the distance. Jeffers pointed again. I watched Leduc put his water bottle and towel on the floor next to a rack of free weights then use a nearby wall to brace himself while he stretched out his quads. There was a door next to where he was stretching, and he inched closer and closer to it so that when it was time for him to switch legs, all he had to do was apply a little pressure on the push bar. The door opened a crack and he was gone.

My jaw dropped and I looked to Jeffers.

"That door opens to a staircase that leads down to maintenance closet and to an outdoor access," Jeffers said. "I don't know if he propped the door open or what, but he returns about an hour later, collects his things and leaves."

"Would he have had time to get to the school? To kill Al? And what about Ellie? She was there around the same time?"

"It's fifteen minutes to the school, give or take. Remember how Ellie said Macie wouldn't let her in the office? Spoke to her from the doorway?"

"Which means Vince could have been inside and Ellie never would have known."

"He would have had a half an hour."

"That's not a lot of time," I said. "And to be fair, we don't even know if that's where he went."

"No, we don't. But we know he went somewhere. And he lied to us about it."

"Can you play it again?" I asked. Jeffers restarted the video. "Pause it there." Vincent Leduc froze midstride on his way to the weight room. "I know the footage is black and white, but check out his shorts. Any chance they could be the blue we're looking for?"

"There's always a chance, Samuel. Unfortunately, there's no way of telling. Can't extract colour from black-and-white digital images."

"They don't look black or white to me."

"To me either. Looks like Leduc has more than just his whereabouts to answer for."

"Do you really think this Vince guy could have done it?" Natalie asked over the phone after Jeffers had eaten me out of house and home and finally left.

"I don't know," I said. "I don't know anything anymore. This case has Jeffers and me going around in circles."

I plopped down on the sofa with a glass of wine and pulled a blanket over me. As soon as Jeffers left, I had removed my pants and thrown them onto Moustache's chair. The dog was fully engaged and fully entangled.

"Did you find out anything more about Laura?"

"She was a vegetarian and not really into mac and cheese."

"What?"

"Nothing. No. I haven't really asked and he hasn't offered."

"Is it still driving you crazy?"

"Not really. Maybe a little."

"Bel?"

"Okay, yes!" I confessed. "It shouldn't! It's a relationship that's way in the past. She's dead, for crying out loud! It shouldn't matter at all!"

"So why does it?"

I shook my head and escaped into my wine glass. It was a very good question for which I didn't have a very good answer.

"Maybe because I want him all to myself," I conceded. "When a relationship ends, the heart eventually lets go of the other person. But when someone dies … there's always a part of them there, you know?"

"That's true," Natalie said. "But, Bel, he's with you now. And you two are making your own memories and writing your own inside jokes. There may always be a shadow of Laura, but a shadow can't compete with you."

"Yeah," I said, not entirely convinced. "But how could they not find her body? I could understand if she'd been murdered. There are a million ways to dispose of a body. But you can't do that to yourself. Can you?"

"Sure you can. Jump into a volcano."

"Natalie—"

"What? Tell me that wouldn't work."

It was actually pretty genius, but highly unlikely in Laura's case.

"Best bet is probably tying rocks around your body and throwing yourself into the water and letting nature eat away at you," Natalie said.

Again the image of the torso sprang to mind.

"I suppose you could encase yourself in concrete," she said. "Or—"

"Okay!"

"Google it, Bel. You can find anything on the Internet nowadays. I bet it's not as hard as you think. Listen, why don't you and Paul come into the city for supper? Zack would love to see you. It's been so long. We can do dim sum!"

It had become a thing, early in our friendship, to gorge ourselves on Chinese food. Toronto's Chinatown was a culinary paradise that was a must-visit whenever I was in the city and one that saw all of my self-control fly out the window.

"I'm not sure I'm ready for Paul to see that side of me," I said, laughing.

"It's all about making new memories, remember?"

I rolled my eyes. "I'll check our schedules."

"Hey," she said. "Maybe it's not so much circles as it is a spiral," Natalie said.

"What?"

"You said before, you felt like you were going in circles."

"Yeah? So?"

"With a spiral, you're still moving in circles, gathering information, but the circles get smaller and smaller until you reach the centre."

"Yeah, but with a spiral, it's a common thing around which everything else swirls. I don't think that's the case here. All of the suspects—the Penners, Vince, Powell—there's no relation. Except Al, I guess."

"And maybe the person who killed him."

"I'm not sure I understa—Oh my god, Natalie. Are you suggesting that all of the suspects know who the actual killer is and that the killer is at the centre of the spiral?"

"They may not know the killer is the killer."

"No. But maybe he's someone they're all connected to in some way."

I ran Natalie's theory by Jeffers the next day as we made our way to the school. It was one of my teaching days and I was resentful. I wanted to be at rehearsal patching things up with Powell. Not to mention actually rehearsing. Previews were approaching quickly and while I had reached a comfortable place in my scene with Eeyore, I was feeling more and more insecure about my impending musical debut.

"I can see how Leduc and the Penners might know some of the same people, but I don't know how Powell Avery would figure in," Jeffers said.

"That's what's tripping me up too. As far as I know, he has no association with the school. Vince has no connection to the hospital or Adele. And we know Armin Penner's view of the theatre. So how can they all possibly be related?"

"Let's not worry about that for now. Let's first get to the bottom of Leduc's little disappearing act and see if that clears anything up."

Vince was in the studio arranging chairs when we arrived.

"Oh good, you're here," he said. His acknowledgment was brief, and he immediately returned his focus to the chairs. "There's a Spirit Day next week and all of the classes with visiting artists have been asked to do a little showcase of sorts at the assembly. I thought we might—" Vince looked up and registered Jeffers' presence for the first time. "Detective."

"If you have a minute?" Jeffers said.

"I don't actually," Vince said. "I have a class starting in five minutes and—"

"The question was just a courtesy."

Vince pursed his lips, pulled a chair out of his careful arrangement, and sat. He indicated that we should do the same.

"The morning Al died, you said you were working out at White Oaks."

Vince smiled sardonically, brought his elbows to his knees, and laid his head in his hands. Eventually he met Jeffers' gaze. He knew he'd been caught.

"You want to tell us where you really were?" Jeffers asked.

Vince took an excruciatingly long pause then, very simply, said, "Here."

"At the school?"

"That's right."

"With Al?"

"Yes. Well, no, not exactly."

"What does that mean?" I asked.

"I came here to see Al, but I didn't."

"Why?"

"Why did I come or why didn't I see him?"

"Both," Jeffers and I said at the same time.

A group of girls, Ellie among them, came chattering into the room. I caught Ellie's eye. She looked away and separated herself from the group.

"Morning, Mr. Leduc. Hi, Bella," one of the girls called.

"Hi, Samara," Vince said. I waved and offered a smile. "Listen, Bella and I need to finish up here. We'll just be a minute. If you guys can get the rest of the chairs in a circle, that would be great. And maybe one of you can lead the class in a warm-up?"

"Sure," said the girl.

Vince nodded his thanks then gestured to Jeffers and me to join him in his office.

"OK," he said, when Jeffers and I were seated. He remained standing, his arms crossed against his chest and the bookshelf taking on much of his weight. "Every year, on the anniversary of Avril's death, I pay a visit to Al."

"Are you saying Al died on the same day as your sister?" I asked. I could see puzzlement on Jeffers' face as well. Neither of us had put the dates together.

Vince nodded. "Irony. Coincidence. Karma. Maybe a little bit of all three ... It wasn't a surprise. My visit. Al expected me. Like I said, I did it every year. I wanted to be sure he never forgot her."

"And what would you do during these visits?" Jeffers asked.

"Nothing really. A bit of chit chat. We'd catch up. Not friendly or anything. It wasn't like that. And it never lasted too long. Seeing me was enough to get him thinking of Avril. Of his part in her death. He was never punished for it. Not legally. This was the only way I could think of to make sure he never got away with it completely."

"You've done this every year for—"

"Twenty-three years. Almost a life sentence."

"Is that why your career seems to have mirrored Al's?" I asked. "Because it was easier to stalk him?"

"It wasn't stalking. I just—"

"How did you know where he'd be every year?" I asked.

"Sounds like stalking to me," Jeffers chimed in.

"We work for the same board! It's not hard to know where people are!" Vince said.

"And how did you come to work for the same board?" Jeffers asked. "What prompted the decision to leave acting and move into education? To relocate to this region?"

"I didn't—. You're making it sound like—"

"Because it *is* like!" Jeffers said.

The two men stared at one another.

"You know what else it sounds like to me?" Jeffers persisted. "It sounds like you gave up your whole life, your whole career to—"

"What about Avril's life?" Vince said, viciously. "What about the career she should have had? The things she wanted?"

"Would she have wanted this?" Jeffers asked.

"Okay. That's enough," I said. I knew Jeffers was trying to drive Vince to the edge so he'd talk, but I was worried he'd gone too far. Jeffers didn't like Vince. He'd made no secret about that. But we couldn't risk losing Vince. Not now. "Can we just focus on the morning Al died?"

"That's why I'm here," Jeffers said, after a moment.

Vince pulled himself away from the support of the shelf and shoved his hands into his pockets. What Jeffers said had clearly hit home. His shoulders slumped and his gaze fell to the floor. "I got here a little after six," he admitted. "Al was in here. He was talking to someone. A man. The door was closed. It sounded a little heated."

"Did you recognize the voice?" I asked.

Vince shook his head. "It sounded like the man was crying."

"Could you hear what they were talking about?"

"No. I waited for a bit. Then I heard someone coming, so I ducked around the corner."

"Why?"

"I don't know. I just didn't feel like seeing anyone."

"Go on."

"It must have been a student. Sounded young. Had a brief exchange with Al. I didn't stick around for all of it. She was upset too. Figures Al would leave a wake of misery."

"Where did you go?" Jeffers asked, ignoring the dig at Macie.

"I was getting impatient and irritated and was on my way back to my car."

"Did you see anyone else at the school?"

"No."

"Dammit," Jeffers said, before he could help himself. The same thought ran through my mind.

The dejected silence in the room was broken by the sound of the students playing the Shakespearean game, Forsooth, in the studio. It had quickly become their favourite warm-up.

"I went back though," Vince said.

"To ... here?" I asked. "To Al's office?"

"When?" Jeffers asked.

"I was on my way back to my car, but I turned around. It was coming up on six thirty. Twenty after or so."

"And?" Jeffers and I said in unison.

"He was dead."

Chapter 24

"At least I thought he was dead. He looked dead."

"Why the hell didn't you tell us any of this?" Jeffers asked, getting to his feet, his voice rising. "Why is this just coming out now?"

"It all would have come out! Everything about Avril! About me and Al! I knew what people would think," Vince replied, matching Jeffers in volume and intensity.

"Do you have any idea—?"

"Shh," I said, indicating the students on the other side of the door. "Give me a minute."

I went into the black box, gathered the students, and asked them to take turns performing their scenes for each other. When I returned to the office, Jeffers and Vince were exactly where I had left them, standing on opposite sides of the room, and mad as hell.

"Let's do this quietly," I said.

Jeffers resumed his seat. Vince glanced at his chair then thought better of it. I stayed somewhere in the middle in case I had to intervene.

"Perhaps you can tell us exactly what you saw," Jeffers said with as much calm as he could muster.

"When I came back to the office, I didn't hear anything. I knocked on the door. There was no answer, but I wasn't going to let him avoid me, so I opened the door." Vince shook his head at the memory. "He was slumped on the floor. There."

Vince pointed to the patch of wall next to the door to the studio, not far from where I was standing. I felt an urge to move but held my ground.

"It was like he'd been sitting against the wall and had fallen over," Vince explained. "I called his name. There was no response."

"Did you go to him? Check for a pulse?" Jeffers asked.

"No."

"You didn't help in any way?"

"I just left. I got out of there as fast as I could."

"How could you do that?" I asked. "Just leave him there. You could have saved him! He might have still been alive!"

"Was he?' Vince looked challengingly at me, then at Jeffers. Jeffers gave a small shake of his head. "Then what does it matter?"

I opened my mouth to speak but realized there was no point in arguing.

"The only thing going through my head was that it was all finally over," Vince said.

"What about all that stuff you just said about what people would think?" I asked.

"That was later. After I'd left. After I'd had a chance to process what had happened. I knew if I came forward I'd have to explain what I was doing there. It would seem as if I had some sort of vendetta against Al—"

"Which you did!"

"Okay. Fine. Maybe. But—"

"Maybe?"

"Bella, let him talk," Jeffers said.

Vince sighed. "Look, I didn't want him dead. I've never wished him any harm. I just thought he should have been punished and I did the only thing I could think of. I realize it sounds crazy. That I sound crazy. To have spent all these years and … given up so much … but … When I saw him lying there, I felt like I got my life back."

An ill-timed smattering of applause drifted in as one of the groups finished their performance.

"Did you see anyone else? Hear anything?" Jeffers asked.

Vince shook his head.

"And you had no contact with the body?"

"No."

"Why all the secrecy?" I asked. "Why go through the whole business of sneaking out of the gym? Why not just come here?"

Vince gave a pathetic laugh. "There's a contest."

"Excuse me?"

"A 30-Day Challenge. You have to show up for thirty consecutive days. I had to sign in and out, otherwise—"

"You've got to be kidding me," I said, unable to hide my disgust.

Vince shrugged and looked away.

"I think we're done here," Jeffers said, and stood to go. "What colour were your shorts?" he added, when he got to the door.

"What?"

"The shorts you wore to the gym that day? The shorts you were wearing when you came here?"

"What does that have to do with anything?"

"It doesn't," Jeffers said with a sigh. "Not anymore. I'm just curious."

"Blue," Vince said.

"Can you be more specific?"

"Royal blue. I bought a package of three at Walmart. $12.99. Do you need to know my size or will that suffice?"

"I'll leave you to your class."

I walked with Jeffers into the hallway.

"You good to stay?" he asked.

"I'm fine. I'll call you later," I said and turned back into the office.

"We good?" Vince asked.

"You mean, can we continue working together?"

He shrugged.

"We're never going to be friends, Vince. I find a whole lot wrong with what you've done. Just because I can understand it doesn't mean I admire it. As for this class, it isn't about either one of us. It's about the kids. So as long as we're straight on that, we're good."

"Then let's get out there."

The green room was abuzz when I walked in. Manda Rogers was standing amid a group of gushing admirers. I rolled my eyes and made my way over to where Adam and Powell had their heads together at a corner table. I could see Adam's hands moving a mile a minute, so I knew he was excited.

"Oh my god, Bella, have you heard?" he asked when I slid in next to him.

"I just got here. What's going on?"

"I can't even," Adam said, breathless, handing the reins of conversation to Powell, who opened his mouth to speak but was bulldozed by Adam. "Manda and Sergei eloped!"

"The director for *Uncle Vanya*?" They both nodded. "I thought she was dating … the Irish guy—what's his name? Brian?"

"Brennan and that was ages ago," Adam said.

"Ages ago? I just saw them together."

"Well, they're not together anymore. Now she's with Sergei and, evidently, they eloped last night."

"Where? One of those drive-thru chapels in Niagara Falls?"

"Elope Niagara." I had been sarcastic but Adam answered in all seriousness. "It's a mini log cabin. Super cute. Technically, it's in Fort Erie."

The Canadian side of Niagara Falls has proudly waved its flag as the "Honeymoon Capital of the World" for decades. Whether or not it was actually true, I had no idea. But there were plenty of Las Vegas-esque chapels and themed motels to support the claim. Some of them even came with Elvis.

I looked to Powell for confirmation that this was actually happening and that I was not in the middle of a crazy dream. He nodded.

"I've got to run but, oh my god, you should see the ring," Adam said, blowing kisses to us as he gathered his things and left.

"Oh, I'm sure I will," I said.

"You can probably see it from here." It was the first time Powell had spoken since I'd joined them. I took it as an olive branch. Although it really should have been me to extend it.

I glanced up at Adam, who mouthed the word "tacky" over his shoulder to us as he passed Manda's outstretched hand.

I laughed and asked Powell if it was really that bad.

"It's orange," he said.

"The ring?"

"I think the official term is 'rose gold.'"

"Well, it will go with her hair in any case."

Manda let out a squeal as the bridegroom entered the room. A few tables broke into applause and Powell and I dutifully followed suit when Manda's gaze landed on us. Her smile was radiant and Sergei looked at her adoringly. I pitied him. He was an attractive man at the height of his career. A mainstay of the Vakhtangov Theatre in Moscow, Sergei caught the attention of the world stage when his production of Pushkin's *Boris Godunov* was given an invitation to play Lincoln Center in New York, and from there, his career skyrocketed. That the Shaw Festival had been able to woo him to Niagara-on-the-Lake to direct *Uncle Vanya* was a theatrical coup that had international tongues wagging.

"So does this mean she's moving to Russia?" I asked, a little too eagerly.

Powell laughed. "Can you imagine?"

"I can't," I said, looking at Sergei's beaming face. This was not going to end well. "Listen," I continued, "about the other day…"

"I'm sorry I flew off the handle."

"No, I'm sorry! I—"

"My relationship with Al has always been very … private. So when you said—"

"And that's why I thought it might be easier to talk to me than the police. But it wasn't my place. I shouldn't have pushed. I feel awful."

"Don't. It's fine. Really," he said and squeezed my hand gently.

"Since we're on the subject, do you mind if I ask you another question?"

He smiled wryly. "Go ahead."

I took a quick glance around the room. Manda was still

holding court with Sergei by her side, but the throng of well-wishers had thinned considerably.

I lowered my voice and leaned into Powell. "Would you be able to tell me where you and Al were that last time you were together? When he called things off?"

He hesitated. "Would that help?"

"It might."

"You can't tell me anything more, can you?"

"I'm sorry."

He ran his hands through his hair and leaned back with his arms across his chest. "The Millcroft Inn." I shook my head. "It's in Caledon. About two hours away."

"And when was this?"

"First weekend in February."

"That was shortly before he died!"

Powell nodded. "A week."

"I'm so sorry. I didn't realize you'd been together as late as that."

A few quick blinks did away with the tears that had formed in Powell's eyes. However one might classify their relationship, Powell and Al had shared something meaningful.

"Thank you," I said, squeezing his hand.

I picked up my phone and texted Jeffers. He responded almost immediately, *You're a goddess, Samuel.* Then followed it with, *You and Doc come for dinner tonight.*

"You coming?" Powell asked, gathering his things.

We had a run-through of *Cabaret.* Our last in the rehearsal hall. We were scheduled to move onto the stage and a full set after this, which would present a whole new world of issues: choreography would likely have to be re-spaced, set pieces would require new negotiation, and backstage traffic would result in countless bruises. And then there was the always problematic addition of stairs and doors. Stage managers always tape out the footprint of the set on the floor of the rehearsal hall, carefully indicating the direction in which doors open and close and defining steps as close to scale as possible. But despite their best efforts, actors all turn into superheroes, capable of walking through closed doors and climbing a staircase in a single bound. Then the set arrives, and they revert to toddlers, as if seeing such things for the first time.

"Powell," I said, my hand on his forearm, "I promise to keep you out of it as best I can."

"Just get whoever did this."

"That's what we're trying to do."

"Honey, we should go here," Aria Jeffers said, as she scrolled through the Millcroft Inn's website. "Look, there's a hot springs! Remember when we were in Banff? You loved the hot springs." She looked to Paul and me, "Andre and I went for a friend's wedding and he almost missed the ceremony because he wouldn't get out of the pool."

"That must be new," Paul said.

"You've been there?" I asked.

"Years ago. It was lovely. Fantastic food."

"How can you even think of food right now?" Jeffers asked, patting his stomach.

Aria had made an amazing turkey casserole that we'd devoured before settling our very full selves in the Jeffers' living room. Jeffers and Aria were sitting together on the sofa and Paul and I occupied the two other chairs that made up the set. An image of Paul and Laura sprang to mind. Which was ridiculous in itself, as I had no idea what Laura had looked like. In my mind's eye, she was perfect in all the places I had flaws and then some.

"Oh, the food does look good," Aria squealed. "Venison strip loin, butter-poached monkfish…"

"Yes, and a forty-seven-dollar puréed beef tenderloin for the baby," Jeffers said.

"We wouldn't bring the baby," Aria said to her husband. "That's the whole point. We could leave the baby with my parents. Have some time. Just the two of us. Remember what that was like?"

As if on cue, the baby monitor sounded. Aria moved the computer to Jeffers' lap with a wistful sigh and gave his knee a loving squeeze before excusing herself to check on their son.

"So…" Jeffers said, hitting keys on the laptop.

"If you guys are going to talk business," Paul said, "why don't I take care of the dishes?"

"Thanks, man," Jeffers said. "We won't be too long. And, hey, can you take the crumble out of the oven?"

"Sure thing."

Paul gave me a wink and disappeared into the kitchen.

"The manager of the inn sent over the guest list from the weekend Al and Powell were there. I have one of the guys running the names." I joined Jeffers on the sofa and looked at the screen. Other than P Avery, none of the names jumped out at me.

"You know, most of these reservations were made and paid for by one person. P Avery, two guests; A Armstrong, two guests; Ralph Carmichael, four guests. There's no way of knowing who the guests are. Al's name isn't there. And maybe one of these guests is the person we're looking for. You're going to interview all these people?"

"Do you have a better suggestion?"

"We don't even know for sure that seeing someone he recognized is what spooked Al. I know it makes sense that

Al would be worried about word getting back to Glynn, but maybe that's not it at all. Not if they had an arrangement. This could all be a waste of time."

"Well, aren't you a negative Nelly all of a sudden."

"I'm not."

"You've been quiet since Paul mentioned he'd been to the inn."

"No, I haven't! He said that, what, five seconds ago! I haven't said anything in five seconds, so automatically I'm—"

"I'm just saying—"

"Shh," I said, gesturing toward the kitchen. I could hear the water running and the clatter of cutlery. "It's nothing. I'm fine. I'm just … frustrated."

"You and me both, Samuel."

"So what now? We see if any of these people knew Al and then what?"

"What if it was the other way around?"

"What?"

"What if that person didn't see Al? What if Al saw them?"

"Isn't that the same thing?"

"Not even close."

Chapter 25

"We should go too," Paul said on our way home from dinner. "Not at the same time as Aria and Jeffers, but…"

"Where?"

"The Inn. You'd love it!" He moved one hand off the steering wheel and moved it to my knee before adding, suggestively, "We haven't really had the chance to get away since we've been together, so …"

"Well … I … work most weekends…"

"We could head up on a Sunday after your rehearsal, spend the day Monday and head back after supper?"

"That would mean you would have to take a day off."

"The clinic would be fine without me for one day." I was silent. "Or, we could wait until your shows are up and running. Might have a bit more flexibility then. Might even be able to get a couple of days away."

"Yeah," I said. "I'd have to find someone for Moustache though."

"I'm sure one of the techs at the clinic would love to take him. They're always doing that."

"I wouldn't want to impose."

"Is everything okay?"

"Of course," I said, taking his hand from my knee and intertwining my fingers with his.

"You know, we don't have to go. If you don't want to."

"I do," I said. Even as I spoke the words, I didn't believe them.

"I just thought it would be nice. I was there for a conference years ago and it sounds like they've—"

"You were there for a conference?"

"Yeah. Canine orthopaedics."

I let out a breath I hadn't been aware of holding and tightened my grip on Paul's hand. He took his eyes off the road and stole a glance at me.

"Bells?"

"Nothing."

"You want to tell me what's going on?"

I didn't. I didn't want to admit to him that I was insanely jealous of his dead fiancée and that, ever since he had mentioned having visited the Inn, my mind had been running an X-rated loop of their romantic escape; that I knew our relationship was happening only because she had died; and that I wondered if he would ever love me the same way.

If? What? How? So many questions sprang to mind. So many assumptions. My insecurities jumped on each one with full force and breathed life into them. I felt my face flush and my hands go clammy at the same time.

"I need to get out," I said, self-consciously letting go of Paul's hand.

"What? We're almost there!"

"Just let me out please. I'm not feeling well."

He pulled onto the shoulder. I was out of the car before he'd even had a chance to put the car in neutral.

"Bells? My god, what is it?" he said, coming around the front of the car to meet me. I was bent over with my hands on my knees.

"I just need some air. I'm going to walk from here."

"We're so close. Just get back in the car. We can roll the windows down. And when we get to your place, we'll grab Moustache and walk around the neighbourhood until you feel better."

"Paul ... I think maybe ... I should just be alone tonight."

"Bella, what's going on?"

"Can we just ... talk about this another time?"

"Talk about what?"

I was silent. He didn't push.

"Okay," he said. "Will you text me when you get home so I know you're safe?"

I nodded.

He made his way back to the driver's side door. "Bells, I love you. Whatever's going on ... You do what you need, but know that."

I nodded again. "I do."

Moustache had built a fort of blankets and cushions on the sofa. One hind leg dangling over the edge was all that gave away his presence. I squeezed in next to him and ran a hand over his belly. He looked at me with sleepy eyes and rolled further onto his back so I could extend my coverage. With my other hand, I pulled out my phone and dialed Natalie.

"What's wrong?" she said immediately.

"Why would anything be wrong?"

"I got a feeling. What's going on?"

I spilled every pathetic detail.

"Bel, jeez," Natalie said, when I'd finished. "Why are you so hung up on this?"

"I don't know!"

"She's gone! It's over! It was a long time ago!"

"I know. I know. I know that. I do. But…"

"But what?"

"It didn't end because it was over. She died. It's different."

"Why?"

"It just is."

We were silent for a few moments. Then Natalie came in, gently, "Bella, you are competing with a ghost. And if you are not careful you are going to ruin this."

I nodded even though I knew she couldn't see me. I had run from intimacy my whole life as a means of self-protection, as a way of avoiding re-experiencing the pain of loss. I had filled my quota by the age of eight, and while my heart had miraculously mended and made room for others over time, I knew its broken pieces had been stitched backed together so loosely that the thread could break at any moment.

"You're using this as an excuse, Bel," Natalie said. "You are feeling so much—maybe too much—and it is freaking you out and you are using Laura as an excuse. None of this is about Laura! None of this is about Paul. This is about you and what you do. What you always do."

"Natalie—"

"You have a wonderful man who loves you. And I can't promise you that it's always going to be perfect and that you're going to live happily ever after. But from where I sit, it's pretty damn good right now. You've had enough hurt, Bel. Try something else on for a change."

After a few more admonishments from her and some promises from me, we hung up. I turned to find Moustache sitting at his full height, staring at me under a furrowed brow.

"I suppose you agree with Natalie?"

The dog gave a snort.

"It isn't so easy for me, you know."

Moustache gave a groan that would have rivalled any human eye roll, lowered himself to his forearms, and laid his head in my lap. His beautiful brown eyes looked up at me, all our years together shining behind them, showing me just how easy it indeed had been for me to open my heart.

I stroked his ears. He wiggled further onto my lap and swatted my phone with his paw.

I fired off a quick text to Paul saying that I'd gotten home safely and that I was sorry.

There was a knock on the door.

"It took you long enough," he said when I'd answered. Moustache jumped up on him, resting his paws on his thighs and bouncing on his hind legs. "I saw you get in and—"

"I'm sorry. I got caught up with Natalie. I know I was supposed to … I'm awful … I should have … I thought you went home," I said.

"Do you really think I was going to leave things like that?" He picked up Moustache's lion and tossed it into the kitchen. The dog flew after it in delight.

"I'm sorry," I said again.

He reached out, took my face in his hands, and kissed me. I could hear Moustache galloping down the hall toward us and, when I opened my eyes, I looked down to find him standing between us, the lion at his feet, his mouth open in a broad smile.

Paul threw the lion again. "May I come in?" he asked.

"Of course," I said, taking his hand and leading him into the living room. "Do you want a drink?"

"No. I want you to tell me what that was all about."

Moustache saw Paul on the sofa, gave up the game of fetch, and ran over to protect his fort. He plumped the pillows, bunched the blanket, and stamped the cushions all before poor Paul could even think about making himself comfortable. With his stake firmly claimed, Moustache stretched out with a snore, leaving Paul with only a small corner on which to sit. He patted the dog's rump and moved to the floor. I joined him, and he wrapped a strong arm around me.

"So...?"

I hesitated. He gave me a gentle squeeze.

"I thought—when you said you'd been to the inn—I thought you were there with Laura and I was ... jealous."

"Bells—"

"I know it doesn't make sense. You have past relationships. I have past relationships. They don't matter. Or they shouldn't, but ... she ... does."

Paul took a deep breath and kissed my head. "She matters to me too. But she's gone. I have come to terms with that and I have moved on."

"How? It took me years after my parents died. In some ways I'm still not over it. How can you have come to terms with it when it's only been a few years?"

"It's been four years and people grieve differently. You know that."

"But—"

"Bella, your parents died tragically. There's no way you could have been prepared for something like that. And at such a young age. It's no wonder it has stayed with you. With Laura it was ... a relief, to tell you the truth. In death, she finally found peace, and I guess I've always been comforted by that. Maybe that's why it was easier for me.

'Easier' isn't the right word, but..." I leaned into him and put my head against his chest. "Bells, I love you. I'm not going anywhere, and I don't wish for things to be any different than they are right now."

A tear rolled down my cheek and I buried my face into him. He held me close and, lulled by the dulcet tones of Moustache's snores, I stayed like that, letting all thoughts of Laura drift away and wishing all thoughts of who killed Al Macie would do the same.

Chapter 26

I was late for my class with Vince. Jeffers had called as I'd arrived at the school to tell me that the samples from the rag I had taken from the Penners' barn had not matched the fibres found on Macie. It didn't rule out any of the Penners, but it meant we had to keep digging.

I was rushing around to the front entrance when I saw a group of boys exiting one of the side doors and decided to sneak in that way and avoid the lengthy security measures I'd have to endure if I went to the main door. I was counting on the boys not being sticklers for the rules. I was not counting on one of the boys being Leland Penner.

He purposely bumped my shoulder as I passed.

"Nice," I said, under my breath.

"You got something to say?" he asked.

"Drop the attitude, Leland."

He laughed, and the other boys started in with some ribbing.

"That's enough," I said in my best teacher voice. "Guys, can you excuse Leland and me for a minute please."

"I got nothing to say to you."

"I said, 'drop the attitude.'" Leland put his best stare on and I did my best not to let it intimidate me. "I am here in an official capacity, which gives me authority. You do not have to like me, but you will show some respect."

"Or what?"

I channelled every ounce of Emma Samuel's tough-as-nails exterior I could muster. I was determined to hold my ground.

"Or I'm sure Principal Harvey can find room for you in his office."

"Ooo-oo," he said, feigning fear. "Mr. Harvey's been friends with Da for years. He's not going to do anything."

"Well then, perhaps I should skip Mr. Harvey and go straight to your dad."

That seemed to do the trick. Leland Penner may have held me, Gerald Harvey, and other elders in little regard, but the threat of telling his father caused a fracture in his foundation. And once there's a crack…

"Fine. I'm sorry for bumping you," he mumbled and turned to join his friends.

"I'm not finished."

He turned back to me with a groan. I had Emma Samuel locked and loaded. There was no turning back.

"You saw someone else. That morning."

"What are you talking about?"

"When Detective Jeffers asked you if you saw anyone else at the school the morning Mr. Macie was killed, you hesitated and looked to your father."

"I didn't mean—"

"Who else was here?"

"I told you—"

"Who else?"

"Dude!" one of his friends called. "Are you coming?"

"We can talk down at the police station if you'd rather," I said, giving my words more weight than they actually had.

"Just go on," Leland said to his buddies. "I'll meet you over there."

His friends headed off in the direction of the McDonald's across the street.

"I didn't see him," he said to me when he was sure they were out of earshot. "I just saw his car, so I assumed he was in the school."

"Mr. Leduc?"

"What? No. He drives that green piece of crap," he said, pointing to a green Honda Civic that had, indeed, seen better days.

"You know what all the staff drive?"

He shrugged as if knowing such a thing was the most natural thing in the world. "Mrs. O'Connell drives the grey dinky car. Mr. Flynn's got the Jeep there. Clementine is Madame Irvine's—"

"Clementine?"

"The orange Matrix. She's a bit crazy."

"Okay, whatever," I said.

"And you drive the Echo."

That he knew what I drove gave me the willies. I crossed my arms over my chest, trying to show him that he didn't scare me, but really it was to steady my trembling hands.

"I'm only interested in whose car you saw," I said.

Leland shoved his hands in his pockets and shuffled his feet. If I wasn't mistaken, he looked frightened.

"Leland, does this person know you saw him?"

"I didn't see him!"

"Of course. I'm sorry. His car." More hesitation. "Has he threatened you?"

"He didn't do anything! He's not that kind of person!"

"All right," I said, changing tactics. "But maybe *he* saw something that could help us. It would be really great if we could talk to him. No one's in any trouble. We can leave your name out of it. We just want to talk to him."

At that moment, the fire alarm sounded, and students began spilling into the hallway and out the doors past us. Leland looked me straight in the eye as he backed away and blended into the crowd.

"So he told you nothing?" Jeffers said when I called to tell him about my run-in with Leland.

"He told me someone else was definitely at the school that morning. That's not 'nothing'!"

"But he didn't tell you who. Not only that, he didn't tell you what kind of car, what colour—"

"It's more than we had, Jeffers. Now we know for sure someone else was involved. It's confirmed! It rules out the Penners, Vince—"

"Where was Leduc's car?"

"What? I don't know."

"He was there that morning. Why didn't Leland see his car too?"

"I … don't know. I don't see how it matters now. We have Vince's story. He didn't do it. And we know there was someone else in the building. And this someone else is very likely Al Macie's killer!" Jeffers was silent. "Am I the only one who thinks this is good news?"

"Are you still at the school?"

The firefighters were still doing their sweep of the classrooms. I was standing off by the side of the road, a little apart from where a number of staff and students had gathered. Some people had managed to grab coats, but most huddled together or bounced on the spot for warmth. It may have been spring, but winter was taking its time packing up its things and moving on out.

"Yes, we're just waiting to be let back in."

"Leland could be lying, which means the Penners are still very much in it as far as I'm concerned," Jeffers said.

"True," I said in resignation. Jeffers had succeeded in deflating my mood.

"And see what you can find out from Leduc. Ask him if he saw any other cars there that day."

"He told us he didn't see anyone."

"Just ask! And ask him where the hell he was parked. If he left his car off-site, someone else might have done the same. From the sounds of it, everyone and his uncle were at the school that morning. I refuse to believe no one saw anyone else. Someone is covering up something."

I caught up with Vince in the hall and made my apologies for having missed the start of class. He was polite and professional but by no means friendly.

"You didn't miss much," he said. "The students had just gotten in their groups for the showcase on Thursday. If you work with one group, I'll stay with the other. I'll do a final rehearsal with them tomorrow and then we're good to go. If that works for you?"

"That sounds good," I said. "And I'll get here early on Thursday to help out."

"It's first thing, so…"

"So it shouldn't be a problem. Listen, before we go in, there's something else I need to ask you."

Vince stopped and threw back his head in frustration. When he spoke it was low and direct. "I have told you everything save what I had for breakfast that day, which incidentally—"

"Where did you park your car?" He looked at me,

incredulous. "When you came to the school that morning, where did you park?"

"Are you kidding me?"

"Vince, it's important."

"I parked over at the McDonald's. That answers the breakfast question too, if you must know."

"Why not here, in the lot?"

"In the event that I got here before Al, I didn't want to give him a heads-up."

"But you said you visited him every year. Wouldn't he have been expecting you?"

"Yes. At some point. But he could never be sure of exactly when. It kept him off guard. Uncomfortable. That was all part of it." An Egg McMuffin with a side of sadism. "What does this have to do with anything? What does it matter where I parked?"

"Were there any other cars parked here? When you walked over from McDonald's, did you notice what cars were here at the school?"

"I…" He stopped. My feeling was that he was going to answer off the cuff but decided, if he was ever going to get Jeffers and me off his back, he'd be better off actually thinking about his response. When he spoke again, there was an authenticity in his words.

"I didn't notice," he said. "Isn't that funny? I was so focused on my intention—so focused on getting to Al—that I blocked out everything else. Meisner would be proud, huh?" He chuckled at the irony.

I believed him. I knew exactly what he was talking about. The narrow vision. Your whole world existing on the head of a pin and that being the *only* thing you're able to see. I knew it well.

***

"Can't Jeffers subpoena him, or whatever it's called?" Paul asked.

"Subpoenas are for court appearances," I said.

"Well, whatever it's called. There must be some official police term for bringing someone in and forcing them to talk."

"Arrest. And even that doesn't guarantee you'll get the information you're looking for."

Paul and I were at the Commons, a park area of sorts on the grounds of what was officially called Butler's Barracks, a national historic site commemorating more than 150 years of Canada's military involvement. While enjoyed primarily by cyclists, rollerbladers, joggers, and those just out for a stroll, there are still several structures—officer's quarters, gunshed, and barracks—on the grounds that are open to visitors during the summer months. It was also the only place in town for dogs to run off leash. And, incidentally, where Moustache had orchestrated my first date with Paul.

Moustache raced up and down the lane, stopping to double back when a scent caught his nose or a tree called to his leg. He was supposed to be giving a lesson in socialization to a Portuguese Water Dog puppy, but he had left the poor pup to fend for herself.

"Technically, no one is obligated to give police any information or assist them in any way with regard to an investigation," I explained, using lingo I'd learned from Jeffers and *Port Authority*.

"But if he knows something … If he's lying?"

"Lying is different. That could be considered an obstruction of justice. But Leland hasn't lied. Not really.

Jeffers thinks he has, but he hasn't said *anything*. Can't be a lie if it hasn't been spoken."

Paul clapped his hands to get Moustache's attention. He ran back, mouth open in excitement, ears flapping, his glorious tail wagging as fast as could be managed. It was a look I loved. So much joy. His plume of a tail drooped as Paul affixed his leash and brought him alongside the puppy. The puppy nipped at him playfully, and Moustache let out a huff.

"Just for a little bit, buddy," Paul said to the pouting dog.

He did this from time to time—engaged Moustache's services to help socialize a puppy that was brought to the clinic by rescue shelters for examination prior to adoption. Moustache was not a good teacher but tolerated the puppies without too much grousing and got one of Paul's home-cooked feasts as a reward. Or, rather, bribe.

"So what's Jeffers going to do?"

"I don't know. He's meeting with Inspector Morris today. It's tricky, especially since Leland is only fifteen."

"And his sister didn't see the car?" I looked at him and stopped walking. "You said he followed her, so it would make sense that whatever he saw she saw too."

"Of course!" I said. I reached up to take his face in my hands and was leaning in to plant a big kiss on him when Moustache yanked at the leash, jerking him away.

Paul and the puppy followed obediently as Moustache pulled toward the base of a tree. The puppy narrowly missed being peed on but was unable to avoid the spray of dirt Moustache kicked in her inquisitive face. She let out a sneeze and plopped onto the ground. Moustache looked up to Paul, who laughed and unhooked the leash with one hand and scooped up the puppy with the other.

"That'll teach you to stick your nose in someone else's business," he said to the mass of brown and white curls.

"Indeed," I said, wiping dirt off her snout.

Moustache darted down the path, relishing his freedom and celebrating the end of his work day.

I thought about what Paul had said about Ellie. He was right. The chances that Ellie saw the car were good. But in order to find out whether she did, Jeffers and I would need to get Ellie alone. And what were the chances of that?

Chapter 27

The school was decked out in maroon and metallic blue and was already bustling with activity when I arrived pre-showcase. Most of the students were in the studio waiting for Vince and me and a last-minute rehearsal. Ellie was not part of the group, and I kept a close eye on the door, expecting her to arrive any minute. She didn't.

Nor, for that matter, did Vince.

I led a brief warm-up and reviewed the plan for the presentation then left the students to their nerves and finishing touches. It wasn't until I'd moved into the corridor that I heard voices coming from Vince's office. Ellie sat slumped against the wall, crying softly. Her red eyes met mine and filled with new tears.

"Ellie, what's going on?" I asked.

"My dad found out I was still taking the class. About the audition. All of it. I don't know how, but he found out." She choked out the words between sobs.

For a split second I contemplated taking advantage of Ellie's weakened state and solitude to ask about the car but, ultimately, goodness prevailed. I gave her shoulder a comforting squeeze and stuck my head into the office.

Vince was mid-sentence. "Mr. Penner, I can assure you, I had no idea. It was not my intention to go behind your back. Had I known—"

"She knew!" Armin Penner fired at me.

Vince's desk separated him from Principal Harvey and Armin Penner.

"You knew Elsbeth was forbidden to take this class," Armin spat at me.

"Armin, Ms. James is a guest artist here," Gerald Harvey said in an attempt to smooth things. "She has no say in—"

"She knew," he said again with such ferocity that I almost took a step back. "Are you the one who's been filling Elsbeth's head with ideas? Encouraging her to defy me—"

"Mr. Penner—" I said.

"—to sneak around behind my back—"

"Ellie was—"

"—to lie to me?"

Vince and Gerald Harvey looked back and forth from me to Armin as if watching a tennis match.

I opened my mouth to speak again but was cut off once more.

"Elsbeth was raised to follow the teachings of the church: to find strength in tradition, commitment to family, and dedication to the faith. It does not include—"

"You know that's not true," I said

"I beg your pardon," Armin seethed.

My mind flashed back to Ellie's room. The flashes of colour. The expressions of a growing personality that were stunted in their infancy. The possibilities boxed up and put in the back of the dark closet.

"Ellie was raised to dream. To express herself. To explore and be inspired. That's not to say she can't still be true to the faith, but Ellie was raised to spread her wings. All of your children were."

"You don't know what you're talking about."

"Mr. Penner, I know Adele's death must have been—"

"How dare you!"

"Mr. Penner—"

"How dare you speak her name."

"And how dare *you* not honour it."

That rendered Armin Penner speechless. He stared at me, mouth agape. If it had been a cartoon, I'd have been able to see the bright red rise in his face and steam would have whistled from his ears.

"Ms. James," Gerald Harvey said gently, "I think that's enough."

It wasn't enough. It wasn't near enough. It was true I hadn't known Adele, nor did I really have any idea what life was like for her family before she died. But from what I had been able to put together—from Leland's anger and Corney's contraband to Ellie's aspirations and Armin's religious conversion—this family had stopped living the moment Adele died. Armin Penner sought comfort deep in the church and escaped, with his children, to a place where Adele had never been. A place that had never known her touch or sensed her spirit. And in doing so he had snuffed out the light—her light—that had shone in all of them.

I told him as much.

For a moment I was afraid. And in that moment, I understood clearly how passion and fury could overtake a person so completely that they might hurt another. Or kill. As Al Macie had been killed.

Armin Penner never took his eyes from me as he grabbed his hat from the desk and backed out of the room.

His rage lingered. I didn't move lest the ability to inflict harm was still within its reach.

Gerald Harvey was wearing a team jersey to show his school spirit and had sweated through the chest. There was fire in his eyes too, but I couldn't place it exactly. There was anger as well as something else. Fear maybe? But not fear of Armin. Fear of what?

Jeffers' phone went right to voice mail. I fired off a text and got an automatically generated response that he was in a meeting.

I was pacing the best I could in a crowd of excited students, checking my phone every half second. I didn't know exactly what information I had to tell Jeffers, but I knew something significant had happened and was hoping his police training would be better equipped to make sense of it than my TV equivalent.

I doubled back on my route and came face to face with Adam and Powell.

"What are you guys doing here?" I asked.

"Showing support," Adam said. He leaned in to kiss both of my cheeks.

"An email went out last night inviting company members to the showcase. Something about fostering the relationship between the Festival and the school and the new Artist-in-the-Classroom program," Powell explained.

"But this is just a Spirit Day presentation. It's not the culmination of the program," I said.

"Well, whatever," Adam said. "We were asked to come, so we came."

"You should see the turnout," Powell said. "You'd think an offer for next season was contingent on attendance."

"This better be good. I'm never awake at this hour. Unless I'm on my way home," Adam said with a wink before going off on a tangent about something else.

I was half-listening, my mind still on the events of earlier. Powell had tuned out too and seemed to be distracted by something in the distance.

"Bella," he said, interrupting Adam, for which he received a playful slap. Adam kept talking. "I need to talk to you," he whispered in my ear.

He was scanning the crowd. I tried to follow his gaze but couldn't keep up. A few of our *Cabaret* cast mates joined us, and Adam directed his story to the new and more attentive audience. Powell took advantage and pulled me aside.

"That weekend Al and I went away. I told you he got weird."

"Yes."

"There was another couple there."

"With you?"

"No. They were on their own. We saw them in the restaurant."

Powell's eyes were still searching the hallway. There were people milling about but most had gone into the gymnasium.

"I didn't get it at the time," Powell continued, "but I think Al must have known them. Or one of them."

This was just what Jeffers and I had guessed. That Al had seen someone he knew that weekend.

"Why do you think that?"

"Because one of them is here."

I spun around, looking in every direction, scanning every face. I looked to Powell. At the same time, my phone rang.

Things seemed to speed up and slow down at once. Adam was at Powell's side pulling him away. Vince was standing with our students motioning to me from the end of the hallway. My phone continued to ring, a photo of Jeffers' face identifying the caller.

Teachers corralled late students, music blared, and maroon and metallic blue swirled together. Amplified voices led the student body in the school cheer and a roar erupted through the gym's doors. The noise. The phone ringing in my hand. I ran.

"Where are you?" Jeffers asked.

I was standing at the top of the stairs that led to the basement. I thought I had retreated to the farthest recesses of the school, but the sounds of the assembly permeated through the walls. I had to cover my exposed ear to hear Jeffers properly.

"I'm at the school. Listen, we were right. Al Macie did see someone at the Inn. Powell just confirmed it."

"Did he tell you who?"

"He didn't get a chance. But whoever it was is here, Jeffers. Now!"

"Go see if you can get a positive ID from Powell. I'm on my way," Jeffers said and hung up.

I turned and felt a hand against my chest. The push sent me flying backwards. The sound of my phone clattering down the stairs was a precursor to the contact my body made against the concrete. It landed at the bottom a split second before me and I registered a face reflected in its cracked screen before I passed out.

Chapter 28

There was something dripping on my hand. Steady drops. One every three seconds. I watched them land and waited until the next one. The counting helped me focus and by the time I'd reached ten, my mind was able to take in more of what was going on. Every ounce of my being ached. I was lying on my side and when I tried to raise myself to sitting, the pain caused my consciousness to waver. Wherever I was, I didn't get here on my own. I was sure I wouldn't have been able to manage it.

I steadied my breath and, through small movements, took an inventory of my injuries. My ribs had taken the worst of it and my mind flashed to Manda kicking up her heels in Sally Bowles' shoes. That image alone helped me summon every bit of strength I possessed and push myself upright. It was like being stabbed by a thousand knives. My stomach lurched, and its contents ended up on the floor.

I was in a boiler room that had seen better days. Rusted pipes and puddles on the floor revealed weaknesses in the lines. I leaned my head back against the wall. The dampness was cool and soothing. I closed my eyes, savouring the relief, and must have fallen asleep because when I opened them again, I was face to face with my attacker.

"I brought you some ice," he said. "And some Advil."

"It's going to take more than that."

"I'm sorry," he said. "I didn't mean for you to get hurt."

"You pushed me down a flight of stairs!"

"I know! But I didn't mean … I didn't think … Are you all right?"

"I need a doctor," I said. It hurt to speak. "I'm pretty sure my ribs are broken." Frankly, I was surprised my neck wasn't too.

He shook his head.

"What do you mean, 'no'?" I asked.

"I can't let you go. Not yet. Not until I figure this out."

He paced the length of the small room, covering the distance in three giant strides. The ceiling was low, and he had to bow his head.

"Mr. Harvey," I stammered.

He raised a large hand in a gesture that called for silence and continued to pace.

"Please."

He rushed over to me and laid his baseball glove of a hand over my mouth and nose. "Shut up," he said.

His fingers stretched over my eyes and through them I could see ice in the blue of his own. The pressure he placed on my face cut off my breath, and I feared it would soon crush my nose. I kicked and writhed as best I could. Tears poured down my face, and I screamed into the leather of his palm.

"I said 'shut up'!"

I clawed at his hand and sunk my nails into his flesh. Only then did he seem to realize he'd been suffocating me.

"Oh my god," he said, pulling away. "Not again. Not again."

He repeated it over and over.

I gulped in air, coughing up what I couldn't immediately take in. My lungs pressed against the broken cage that surrounded them. The pain was excruciating, and I passed out again.

"What did he tell you?" he asked when I woke. He had been waiting.

"Who?" My breathing had settled into something manageable, but the pain had not.

"That man! The one at the assembly!"

"I don't know who—"

"You were talking to him! He saw me and whispered something to you!" he yelled.

My brain ached from being jostled during the fall. And the deprivation from oxygen. I brought my hands to my head and willed it to focus. "Powell," I said, as clarity began to settle.

"What did he tell you?"

"Just that he recognized someone."

He stopped pacing and stared at me. His mouth was open, as if he wanted to speak but didn't know the words.

"Bella!" Jeffers called from the other side of the door.

"I'm here," I said, before another of Gerald Harvey's hands could stop me.

"Are you all right?"

I looked to Harvey. He seemed paralyzed. "I'll be fine."

"Mr. Harvey," Jeffers said, "I need you to open the door."

Silence.

"Mr. Harvey—"

"I can't do that," he said.

"It's just me out here. I want to see that Bella's okay."

"I said 'no'!" he roared. His voice bounced off the walls and the reverberation rattled my already compromised bones.

Jeffers was silent. I didn't know if he'd gone. I didn't know a lot of things: how long I'd been down there; what Gerald Harvey's plans were; why he had pushed me in the first place. Things weren't adding up.

"Mr. Harvey," Jeffers called, instilling as much calm as he could. "I'm going to sit out here by the door. It's late. Everyone's gone home. No one else is here, okay? I just want to talk. That's all."

I wondered how late it was. And just how much consciousness I'd lost. I'd missed rehearsal and the implications of that gave me a new kind of headache.

Gerald Harvey still looked perplexed. Since Jeffers arrived, he'd barely moved.

"I spoke with Powell Avery, Mr. Harvey. He was a friend of Al's. He told me he saw you at the Millcroft Inn the weekend before Al died. Do you remember?"

Harvey remained still, his eyes glazed and focused on nothing in particular. My jaw dropped.

"You were the other couple?" I asked, as the pieces slowly fell into place.

Harvey's eyes twitched but remained fixed.

"You and your wife?"

"Not his wife, Bella," Jeffers said.

A tear fell from his eye and got lost in the folds of his neck.

The words penetrated my miraculously resilient skull and began to fill in the blanks of the story. The Millcroft Inn seemed to be the hot spot for infidelity. It was starting to make perfect sense why Harvey and Al would have reacted so strongly to seeing one another. Both having affairs. Both afraid of their respective partners finding out. But it still didn't answer what it was that would have made Gerald Harvey angry enough to kill Al. In my opinion, the playing field was level. They both had information that could hurt the other. Why not agree to pretend nothing happened and leave it at that?

I voiced my confusion to Mr. Harvey and was answered with a blank look.

"Bella, he wasn't there with another woman," Jeffers said. "Mr. Harvey, you were there with a Christopher Neary, isn't that right?"

Chapter 29

Harvey's knees buckled. He steadied himself against the wall and seemed to hold on for dear life.

"Jeffers?" I asked, sure I was missing something.

"I've spoken to Mr. Neary," he said, addressing the principal. "He told me the two of you have been in a relationship for the last fifteen years."

Unable to stay upright, Harvey slid to the floor, tucked his knees into his chest and leaned against the wall. There was something sad about seeing such a large man in such a childlike position.

"Mr. Harvey," Jeffers continued, "you need to talk to us now. You need to tell us everything that happened. We know you didn't mean to kill Al. That it was an accident."

Covering it up and making Al's death look like a suicide was certainly no accident any more than pushing me down the stairs was. Gerald Harvey was in a lot of trouble, but I knew Jeffers was trying to engage his trust, so I kept my mouth shut.

It was a long time coming but, finally, Harvey spoke. "Christopher and I ... We played football together. There was a league. Just a local thing, a few teams. I was engaged to Marnie at the time. I had ... been with men before but ... Every time I was with a man I swore it would never happen

again. Disgusting. There was no way I was gay. I loved
Marnie. It was just … Anyway, I met Christopher and it
was … it."

"But you went ahead and married Marnie," I said.

"Of course I did. Marnie and I had a life. We were best
friends—are! We had plans. Our families … She's a good
woman. I fought my feelings for Christopher for a long
time. It devastated him. He'd been out for a while.
Couldn't understand how I could hide like that. We fought
a lot. He went on to other relationships … But we kept
coming back to each other. Eventually, it settled into what
was. We found time to be together. And it worked for us
for fifteen years."

"You know you're not alone," I said. "There are a lot of
gay men who've married women, often happily, and—"

"That's what Al said."

"Is that what you argued about?" Jeffers asked. "The
morning he died?"

"Al didn't know … how it was with me and
Christopher. He didn't understand. No one did. And if
Marnie…" He choked on a sob. "I went to his office."

"Is this a bad time?"

*"Gerald. Please, have a seat. I … uh … I guess we
should talk about—"*

*"There's nothing to talk about. That's why I'm here. I
want to make that perfectly clear."*

"But—"

*"What you saw—what you think you saw—wasn't …
isn't …"*

"Gerald, please sit down. I can see you're upset."

"I'm not upset, and I don't want to sit!"

"Gerald?"

"I'm not like you!"

"Gay?"

"I love my wife!"

"There are a lot of men who marry women even though—"

"I love my wife!"

"Gerald, calm down. I'm not suggesting—"

"And what about you? What were you doing there? Who was that? It wasn't Glynn. How dare you judge me!"

"I'm not judging. Believe me. Okay? Let's just sit down and ... talk. Maybe it will help."

"Help?"

"Gerald, sit down."

"I don't need any help. What I need is for you to ... promise you won't say anything."

"I—"

"Promise me!"

"I promise. But—"

"I ... we ..."

"Gerald, let me help you to the chair so you can catch your breath."

"Don't touch me!"

"There was a knock on the door. Ellie Penner. She was angry. I didn't know what it was about. I do now, of course. Their private lessons. Al was abrupt with her. She left even more upset than she was when she got there."

"Where were you when Al was talking to Ellie?" Jeffers asked.

"By the door to the studio. She didn't see me. I made sure of that."

For a while no one spoke. The sound of the drips from the leaky pipes arranged themselves in a new age musical composition that underscored the silence.

"It sounds like Al had no intention of telling anyone about you and Christopher," Jeffers said at last.

"I couldn't risk it."

"So you killed him?"

Harvey charged the door. "It was an accident! You said that yourself! You said there was proof of that!"

Jeffers had been trying to get a rise out of Harvey and it had worked.

"You're right," Jeffers said. "I'm sorry."

From what I could tell, Jeffers was using a modified version of cognitive dissonance to unsettle Harvey and throw him off balance. A lot of psychological manipulation goes into police interrogation to bring about a sense of discomfort in whoever is being questioned. Much of this is brought about by how the physical environment is controlled and, as Jeffers and I were clearly at a disadvantage in that regard, I guessed that this was his way of toying with Harvey's sense of power.

"Perhaps you can tell us how it happened," Jeffers suggested. "This accident."

The large man resumed pacing. And sweating.

"Gerald," I said gently, "Earlier you said 'not again'. What did you mean?"

"Like ... before. With you. I didn't realize he couldn't breathe."

"Al, you mean?"

"Ellie left. Al started talking about his own experience."

"Gerald, I understand. I've been where you are. I know about having to lie and pretend and sneak around. About fearing for my job, enduring hateful remarks, missing out on opportunities ... I am judged every day. It's astonishing to me that such discrimination is still so alive and well in this day and age, but it is. So much hatred. So much fear. So little understanding."

"We are not the same! You know nothing about me!"

"All I'm trying to say is that you're not alone. And if you ever want to talk—"

"I don't want to talk! I don't even want to look at you!"

"Gerald, I wish you would sit. I'm worried about you. You don't look well."

"He came toward me again and I pushed him against the wall. He didn't fight me. It was like he knew I just needed to get it all out of my system and then I'd be fine. Like waiting out a child having a tantrum."

"You disgust me! I used to be envious. I used to look at you and see everything I wanted to be. I'd see you and Glynn at things, out and happy, and I'd imagine it was me and Christopher. I'd wish it! You don't need to tell me about the struggle, the captivity of the closet. I know it all too well. I've lived it longer than you. And I have to keep living it. But you are free. And you piss on it by having affairs and going to inns and risking everything. Do you have any idea how lucky you are? To have someone you don't have to hide anything from? To be able to be the person you're meant to be? I have that for one weekend every month. But you have it every day! Don't you know what a gift that is?"

Silence.

"Do you?"

"What did he say?" I asked.

Harvey shook his head. "He couldn't say anything. I didn't realize it but my arm had been under his chin. I had held it there while I'd been talking."

"You crushed his windpipe," Jeffers said.

"I just wanted him to be still. I wanted to be sure he listened. I didn't mean to." Harvey started to cry. "He had my tie in his hands. I think he must have been pulling on it to get my attention, but..."

"Your tie," Jeffers said, "do you happen to recall what colour it was?"

"What?"

"Nothing. Never mind."

We didn't need Harvey to confirm that his tie had been aquamarine. It didn't matter anymore.

"Mr. Harvey, I need you to open the door now." Jeffers' voice was soothing. Trying to lull Harvey into a compliant state.

"What's going to happen?"

"I'm going to make sure Bella is all right. Then we're going to go down to the station and we're going to talk some more."

"I've told you everything."

"Yes. But we still have to talk about what happened after."

"I know I shouldn't have done that. I should have come forward. I panicked."

"You'll have a chance to explain all that."

"I'm in trouble, aren't I?

"Mr. Harvey, open the door."

"Am I going to be arrested?"

"Mr. Harvey."

"What will happen to me? Oh my god. Everything will come out. Marnie. Oh my god."

"Open the door, Gerald!" Jeffers was banging on the door from outside.

I started to pull myself toward the exit.

"I love him, you know. He is my everything. Oh my god. What have I done?"

"Gerald!"

"What have I done to them? Oh my god. Oh my god. You can't tell her. Please don't tell her. Oh my…"

It sounded like Jeffers was using something on the hinges of the door. I picked up my pace. Crawling toward him. My mobility was hindered by my injuries and I hadn't covered much distance when I saw Harvey reach around his back.

"No!" I screamed.

Chapter 30

The gunshot echoed through the boiler room.

"Bella!" Jeffers yelled. His pounding on the door became harder and faster.

I started to hyperventilate.

"Bella, can you hear me?"

I let out some kind of wail that seemed to suffice as a response.

"Move away from the door. I'm going to shoot the lock. Do you understand?"

I nodded but realized he couldn't see that. "Y-es," I managed finally and pulled myself out of the door's path.

"Are you ready?"

"Do it," I yelled, covering my ears with my hands and flattening myself against the wall.

There was a shot. The door opened with a bang. And then there was Jeffers.

"Are you all right?" he asked, taking me by the shoulders and looking me square in the face. I burst into tears, and he pulled me to him. He stroked my hair gently. "Breathe with me," he said and began taking deep breaths. I tried to follow. After about five, I was breathing on my own. He didn't loosen his hold until I reached ten.

He kept one arm around me and I leaned against him, letting him rock me like a child while tears streamed down my face. We sat like that, staring at Gerald Harvey's brains on the pipes and his lifeless body beneath them, listening to the sound of sirens growing louder.

The paramedics agreed with my assessment of broken ribs and were readying me for transport to the hospital for confirmation. I had initially refused, knowing ribs typically heal on their own and that little could be done for them medically but was informed that X-rays were necessary to determine the severity of the fractures.

"Not to mention any jagged edges," Paul said, joining me in the back of the ambulance. "We don't want any of your organs or major blood vessels to be damaged."

"I'm so happy to see you," I said.

He took both my hands in his and kissed my forehead.

"Jeffers filled me in. How are you doing?"

My tears started anew.

"Based on the fall you took, it's best to do a full body scan, just to be sure nothing else is broken," a female paramedic said.

"What about a head CT?" Paul asked. "She could be bleeding internally. Or have a fractured skull or even—"

"I don't have a fractured skull," I said.

"How do you know? You fell down a flight of stairs!"

"I didn't *fall*. I was pushed."

"It's the same thing," he said. "Are you dizzy at all? Do you have a headache? Are you nauseous? Are your arms or legs numb?"

"Paul."

"She lost consciousness," he said to the paramedic. "Did she tell you that?"

"We are aware," said the paramedic, "and we will make sure Ms. James gets all the tests she needs once we get to the hospital."

"She could be hemorrhaging. You've heard of 'talk and die' syndrome, right?"

"I assure you, Mr.—"

"Doctor."

"Don't listen to him," I said. "He's a vet."

"I'm still a doctor."

"I know that, honey. And if I were a cocker spaniel, you'd be the expert here. But I'm not, so please, be quiet and let this lady do her job."

The paramedic smiled. "It's all right, Ms. James. He's just worried about you. To put both your minds at ease, there is a full battery of tests waiting. If there are injuries hiding in there, they won't stay hidden for long."

"Okay?" I directed to Paul.

He nodded and brought my hands to his lips.

"I'm sorry," I said, as fresh tears sprang to my eyes. "I promised you nothing would happen."

"Shh. It's all right. You're okay and that's what's most important."

"Doctor, we're going to head out. Are you going to ride with us or...?"

"I'll follow. We'll need a car at the other end."

"Moustache needs his dinner," I said.

"It's all taken care of. He's fine. Just waiting for you to get home."

"Thank you."

"He asked me to give you this so you wouldn't be scared." He pulled Moustache's lion out of his pocket. I laughed and held it close to me. "I'm going to be right behind you."

***

I was discharged with three broken ribs, a bag of Epsom salts, and a bottle of painkillers. Bruises had formed, and I was told to expect quite a bit of aching and stiffness for the next few days at least. I knew I'd been lucky. I could easily have sustained irreparable damage. Or worse.

Moustache couldn't contain his excitement when I walked through the door. His wiggle propelled him into the air and he launched himself at me. Paul intercepted and bore the brunt of the welcome to spare my body further trauma. But the dog would not be swayed. He deftly sidestepped Paul's interference and found me. Raising himself on his hind legs and resting his front paws on my thighs, he wagged his tail and opened his mouth in one of the biggest smiles I'd ever seen from him.

There are people who say dogs don't "get it," that they don't love us in the same way. They don't understand. Moustache may not have known exactly what had happened, but in that moment, there was not a doubt in my mind that he understood exactly what I needed. Maybe not the catapult of himself but everything else.

"I'm going to run a bath for you," Paul said, leaving me sitting in the hall with the dog snuggled tight against me.

Jeffers appeared in the open doorway. "I stopped by the hospital and they told me you'd been released. Obviously everything checked out?"

He sat down on the floor across from me. Moustache snorted a greeting in his direction but did not budge from my side.

"I'll have my dancing shoes on again tomorrow morning."

"You're not going to take a few days?"

There was no way I was going to let Manda near Sally.

"The show must go on," I said. "It's fine. I called both of my directors from the hospital. It doesn't really affect *On the Rocks*, but I wanted him to know anyway. As for *Cabaret*, I'm not going to go full out and as long as I'm careful, I will be perfectly fine by the time we preview."

Jeffers ran his fingers through his hair and leaned his head back against the wall. We hadn't really had time to talk about anything. When the police and paramedics arrived at the school, they had found us huddled together in the boiler room. I gave a statement and was hurried into the ambulance, and Jeffers immediately took charge of the scene.

"I didn't even consider Harvey," Jeffers said.

"Me neither."

"I was so focused on Vince and the Penners and ... I should have thought. I mean, he was always so nervous when I saw him."

"Nerves aren't always an indication of guilt. You know that."

"But they were! In this case, they were! And I missed it! And ... God ... look at you!"

"Jeffers, I'm fine."

"You're not fine, Bella! You're battered and bruised. You could barely move when I found you."

"How did you find me?"

"I followed Harvey. You weren't answering your phone when I got to the school, so I sought out Vince figuring you'd be with him. He's pissed with you, by the way. Said you were supposed to help with the students but were off with your Festival friends."

"Thanks for the heads-up."

"Anyway, he pointed them out to me. That's how I met Powell. He told me about Harvey. Well, provided a description anyway. When I couldn't find him, or you, I put two and two together. I hung around the school, waiting for him to show himself, and when he finally did … You must have been down there for hours."

"It's okay."

"You keep saying that, but Jesus, Bella, a man killed himself right in front of you!"

I reached out and took Jeffers' hand. "Look at me."

He shook his head. "Bella—"

"Look at me," I repeated. He did. "Physically, I'm going to be fine. And I know I should see somebody to talk about what happened, so, eventually, I will be fine about that too."

"I did this to you. I put you in this situation. Again."

"Gerald Harvey put me in this position. Not you."

"You know what I mean."

"I know you saved me. Again." He squeezed my hand. "We're a team, Jeffers. A few broken ribs isn't going to change that. I don't care what Morris or anyone else says." He smiled. "Now tell me what's going on."

"The school is going to be closed for a few days. I don't know how much is going to be public, but I don't see how the department can spin this, to be honest. I imagine the official story will be suicide. Whether they decide to tie it to Macie's death remains to be seen. We'll keep you out of it if we can."

"I had no idea he had a gun."

"It was registered just a couple of days ago. My guess is the guilt was getting to him and he had started thinking about a way out."

"Have you talked to his wife?"

"She's devastated, as you would expect. She told me she's known about Christopher for years."

"Really?"

"They'd met a couple of times at the football games. She'd never been able to put her finger on it exactly, but she said she could sense something whenever she saw them together. Didn't seem surprised when I told her about their relationship. She had long suspected there was someone else. She said Harvey would go away every month or so for various conferences or whatnot. Always came back from those weekends a different man. Happier, she said. All the same, they had a good marriage. Whatever those weekends were, she knew they were important to him, so she gave him those moments. Because she loved him. She's with Christopher now. She insisted I call him immediately and that he come to the house. They'd both lost the man they loved, and she felt they should be together."

"That's … amazing!"

"That's love," Paul said from the stairs. "Your bath is ready."

Jeffers helped me up. "I'll check on you tomorrow," he said. "I've got a bunch of paperwork to do, but I want to head over to Glynn's at some point. Fill him in. It's better for him to hear it from me than someone else."

"Are you going to tell him about Powell?"

"I haven't decided. It might be enough to say Al saw Gerald and Christopher somewhere and leave it at that. What do you think?"

"I'd like to think everyone is as accepting and as loving as Harvey's wife, but … It's tricky. I know we should probably tell him the whole truth. But maybe there are parts of the whole truth that are better left out, just for the sake of compassion. I've said it before—this is the foundation on which the last twenty years of his life were built. What's to gain if we destroy that?"

"What if he finds out some other way?"

"How would that happen? Al's dead. Gerald's dead. Christopher isn't going to say anything. Powell wouldn't dare. No one else knows."

"Do you know that for sure?"

"I…"

"Lies always come to light. In time."

He was right about that.

"I'd love to tag along," I said.

Paul inhaled deeply. I knew he was swallowing his words. I also knew they'd make their way back up before long and that there was a conversation in the making that I would not be able to avoid. Not tonight though. And I was grateful. I kissed his cheek as I made my way up the stairs. Moustache was glued to my ankles. I reached the bathroom and could hear the boys speaking in hushed tones below. Whatever Paul hadn't been able to say to me was spewing forth to Jeffers, I was sure. I contemplated rescuing Jeffers but didn't have the energy. Instead, I slipped into the bathroom and into the warm water. I surrendered to it, letting the heat and Epsom salts do their magic, while Moustache bunched up the bath mat so he could curl up next to me.

Chapter 31

The pews at St. Mark's Anglican Church were filled by hundreds of people wishing to pay their last respects to Gerald Harvey. Even though the school planned to hold a special assembly honouring him when classes resumed, I recognized many of the staff and students in the congregation.

His death was confirmed as a suicide, but no further details would be released until after the funeral at the request of both Harvey's and Al Macie's families. The community was abuzz with rumours as to what the reasoning might have been, and I'd heard whispers about everything from Harvey being terminally ill to his struggling with depression. There was nothing yet to tie him to Al Macie's death. But there would be. At the moment, however, the present company was there to sympathize rather than speculate and Harvey would have a chance to be remembered for all the wonderful things he had done and had been before the shadow was cast.

"You're looking better," Glynn Radley said, as he joined me and a throng of others standing at the back of the church. The colour around my eyes had started to change from deep blue to greenish-yellow and was, therefore, much easier to disguise with makeup. To anyone who asked, my injuries were the result of a car accident.

News had spread quickly throughout the Festival, and Manda Rogers had practically wet herself in excitement when I hobbled into rehearsal bruised and broken. She didn't have the acting skill to feign sympathy nor to cover her disappointment when I buckled my character shoes and took my place centre stage. Wobbly, but determined.

A chosen few knew the truth. I told Powell and Adam. And Jeffers had told everyone involved with the investigation—Armin Penner, Vince, and, of course, Glynn.

"I'm surprised to see you here," I said.

"I debated coming," Glynn admitted.

"What convinced you?"

"I don't know. I tried to tell myself it's what Al would have wanted. I told you he always saw the good in everyone. Never held a grudge. But … I actually don't think it's about Al. I think I needed something."

Jeffers and I had visited Glynn the day after Harvey's confession and death. In the end, we told him everything. All about Al and Vince's past. All about Powell. All about Al's last moments. He thanked us and asked us to leave.

"Did you get it?" I asked.

"I'm not angry anymore," he said. "I guess that's something." I looked at him, puzzled. "I'd always known Al had … others. And he knew I knew. We never talked about it. We were together for twenty-one years. Together for everything that mattered. And unless I was working, he always came home to me. Why ruin that? Still, having it confirmed … hearing that it was more than a one-night thing, that…"

"I'm sorry. Were we right to have told you?"

He nodded. "And look at that." He jutted his chin at the pew where Harvey's wife and Christopher Neary sat together, hand in hand.

They'd both given eulogies. Harvey's wife had introduced Neary as a "dear friend" and I suppose no more needed to be said nor should have been. It was not the time for that.

"I still don't understand why he wouldn't have told me about Vince. It doesn't make any sense. But I guess I'll never know."

"Maybe that was his cross to bear. Alone."

"Maybe."

The closing hymn's final chords rang out, and people began to file out of the church. Glynn turned to go.

"How's Edith?" I asked.

"She's getting used to things, I guess. We all are. She's taken to sleeping on Al's side of the bed and, to be quite honest, I'm glad to have her there."

I watched Glynn descend the steps then turned to find Armin Penner at my side. He was wearing a suit that was more fashionably tailored than traditional.

I braced myself.

"Ms. James," he said, "I was hoping you'd be here." He recoiled a little at my appearance but had the grace not to say anything.

"Mr. Penner, I really don't think this is the place for—"

"I owe you an apology." My jaw dropped. "But you're right. This is not the place. Perhaps you can come by the house later. Elsbeth is making chicken with bubbat."

"Bubbat?"

"Raisin bread that is baked inside the chicken while it's cooking."

I hesitated. I was curious about the apology, and the bubbat to be honest, but it seemed a little quick to move from where we had last left things to dinner.

"Or perhaps just some tea," he said, reading my mind.

I nodded. "Tea would be lovely."

Ellie opened the door, all smiles, and led me down the hall.

"Ah, good," Armin said upon seeing me.

He had never expressed joy at my presence, and I couldn't remember the last time I'd seen Ellie smile. The whole thing was beginning to feel like an episode of *The Twilight Zone*. I looked out the living room window expecting to see a gremlin setting fire to the house or wreaking some other kind of havoc. I wasn't too far off. Leland was outside loading a wagon with Corney. He caught my eye and looked away quickly.

"Please sit," Armin said, indicating an olive-green wingback chair.

Ellie pretty much skipped out of the room and returned moments later with a full tea service and a plate of cookies. Only then did it register that she was wearing pants. My gaze shot to where Armin sat on the sofa; he was in his usual black pants and white collared shirt, but there was something different about him.

"Have you ever had these?" Ellie asked, holding out the plate to me and interrupting my study of her father. I shook my head. "They're cream cookies. Da made them. They're way better than mine. Whenever I make them, they fall apart."

My face expressed surprise before I had a chance to self-edit. Armin Penner seemed very rigid in his ideas of what constituted "women's work." Baking cookies was surely near the top of that list.

"I know my way around a kitchen, Ms. James," Armin said, reading my mind for the second time that day. "I was one of five boys and there was no way my grandmother would let all of her recipes go to the grave with her. She passed along her most cherished ones to me and my brothers and would not rest until we could make them absolutely perfect. These cookies are a staple in most Mennonite homes, and everyone has an old recipe that's been handed down through generations."

I took one of the cookies. It was round and white with a white glaze and sprinkled with shredded coconut. I bit into it and was surprised by how soft it was. It was the perfect amount of sweet and I contemplated reaching for another, but the image of my costume for *Cabaret* flashed in my mind and stayed my hand.

"My mom taught me her recipe," Ellie said. "She used to put coloured icing on hers. Pink for me, blue for Corney, and green for Lee. But we all liked Da's better. Even Mom. He hasn't made them in a long time though."

"No," Armin said with a touch of sadness.

If I were to guess, I'd say he hadn't donned an apron since Adele's death.

"Ms. James," Armin began, "you said some very hurtful things—"

"You shaved." I blurted out the words and they caught all three of us by surprise.

Armin's hand went to his chin where his long beard had been neatly trimmed into an extended goatee that Sean Connery would have envied. Ellie stifled a giggle.

"I'm so sorry," I said.

Armin smiled shyly and said, "Elsbeth tells me I look like George Clooney."

"Most definitely," I said, smiling back.

He blushed slightly. It was charming. *He* was charming. I had the feeling I was finally meeting the man Adele had loved.

"Ms. James, I gather you have experienced a great loss."

It wasn't a question, so I didn't go into detail. I merely nodded.

"The way you spoke to me in Mr. Leduc's office could only have been born out of empathy. Of having survived something similar. It was hard to hear. I imagine it was also very hard for you to say. I am grateful to you. As I'm sure you are to whomever said those words to you in your time of darkness."

I thought of Natalie. And of a blustery day when I'd been particularly horrible and she'd finally had enough. She'd wielded some pretty tough love. And I pushed her away because of it. Eventually her words sunk in and I realized that I'd spent my entire life pushing people away because it was easier to do that than to get close to them and lose them. Slowly, my heart began to open. But it took time. And I wasn't fully there yet. There were days when I still wanted desperately to close up shop, wrap a chain around my heart, and throw the key somewhere, fathoms deep.

"I heard a saying once, 'You just keep living until you're alive again,'" Armin said. "I dismissed it at the time. But I think I understand it now."

The words hit me like a ton of bricks, and I struggled to keep my composure.

"I couldn't bear a single day without Adele. And I could see her in everything the children did. Things they said, dreams they had … So I took those things away. I robbed them of their very essences because of her presence. I was weak."

"You were grieving."

"Call it what you will, Ms. James. It doesn't excuse the act."

"There's no rule book for grief, Mr. Penner. It's different for everyone. And we do what we must to get through. You would have found your way eventually whether or not I said anything."

"Be that as it may, I still owe you an apology. I have behaved rudely to you and, I daresay, I may have even frightened you. I do hope you'll accept."

"Of course!"

"I owe much more to my children. And to Adele. There are amends to be made. Years to repair." Ellie reached out and took her dad's hand. He pulled her close to him and kissed the top of her head. "So, for starters, I understand that my daughter has a pretty important audition coming up."

My eyes widened in surprise and I looked to Ellie, who sat beaming in her father's embrace.

"Perhaps you can educate an old man on what she's getting into? Life as an actor?"

"I'll do my best," I said, my smile mirroring Ellie's.

I left, making promises of free tickets and backstage tours. Ellie was excited, and Armin was smiling but anxious. While I couldn't imagine doing anything else for a living, it was not an easy lifestyle and I didn't sugar-coat it for either of their sakes. It was a way of life that was financially unstable, emotionally taxing, and a rollercoaster ride from which your self-esteem and confidence could never get off. It is a calling. And when you're doing what you love, all the challenges disappear and there is nothing better in the world.

Ellie had the talent. There was no doubt about that. Whether or not she had what it took to go the distance, I didn't know, but I was glad she was going to get a chance to find out.

Leland was waiting by my car. I took a deep breath, determined not to let him intimidate me.

"Can I help you with something?" I asked.

"Is it true?"

"What?"

"What that cop said about Mr. Harvey. That he killed Ellie's teacher."

I knew Jeffers had informed Armin. I was surprised Armin had shared the information with his kids.

"Leland—"

"It was his car. Mr. Harvey's. It was his car I saw at the school that day. I told Da. After that day in the barn. He said not to tell. That Mr. Harvey couldn't have been involved."

"It was an accident," I said. "Mr. Harvey didn't mean—"

"Did he do that to you?"

I wasn't sure how much Jeffers had told Armin or, subsequently, how much Armin had passed along, so I stayed silent, hoping Leland wouldn't press it.

"My mom and Mr. Harvey's wife were real close. When Ma died, and Da ... they were really good to us."

"Is that why you didn't want to say anything?"

Leland's gaze fell to the ground and his shoulders slumped. "What's going to happen to him?"

"What do you mean?"

"It's going to come out. In the papers, right? What are people going to think? His reputation..."

"I don't know."

"If it was an accident, then he's not a murderer. Right? But people are going to think that anyway."

"Is that what you think?"

"No."

"Then why are you so sure that's what other people will think?"

"Because…"

"Leland?"

He shuffled his feet and kicked at the wheel of my car.

"Because that's what we all think of the doctor who killed Ma," Corney said. He was sitting on the front stoop of the house. I had no idea how long he'd been there.

"She—" Leland started, fire in his eyes and hatred in his voice. "It's isn't the same!"

"Why not?"

"Because it's … she … fuck you, Corney!"

Leland slammed his hand on the window of my car. I waited for it to shatter. It didn't. Thank goodness. He stormed off toward the barn. Armin had a lot of work to undo and a lot of healing to bring about. Ellie and Corney would be amenable, I gathered, but he was going to have his hands full with his youngest.

I looked at Corney. He shrugged, pulled some earbuds out of his pocket, and plugged himself into his own little world.

Chapter 32

"This is for you," Jeffers said, handing me a sealed envelope. "It's from Inspector Morris."

"Oh no. Is it a restraining order? Instructing me to stay at least a thousand feet away from you and any ongoing investigation?"

Jeffers chuckled.

It was a letter of commendation. I looked to Jeffers. "What's this for?"

"For what it says. Read it."

"'The purpose of this letter is to formally commend Campbell James for her exceptional assistance to the NRP'—He had to use Campbell?" I was named after my father's father and it was always the name used when I was in trouble. Maybe this was Morris' way of shaking a finger at me.

"I like it. I wanted him to put Emma Samuel, but he wouldn't go for it."

The letter went on to paint a glorified picture of my involvement in the case. By the time I got to the end, even I was impressed.

"Aren't these things usually given out at some kind of official banquet?"

"Yep. But you don't get to go to that."

"Why not?"

"Because it's a secret, remember? We promised to keep you out of the news?"

"I could have just gone for the meal. Kept my mouth shut." Actors always love free food.

"Here," he said, pulling a paper Starbucks bag out of his coat pocket. "Here's your meal."

"A half-eaten croissant? Oh, Jeffers, you do spoil me."

I pulled off a flaky, buttery piece with my fingers and put it in my mouth. Moustache was instantly at my feet.

"Um … I'm going to need the rest of that back," Jeffers said.

"What?" I mumbled through chews.

"I didn't have breakfast and I've got a bunch of meetings."

"No way! This is my banquet!" I said, holding the croissant above my head and running around the kitchen island.

"Oh, come on," Jeffers said, giving chase.

Moustache bounced on his hind legs, barking in delight.

A long honk from a car horn stopped us in our tracks. Moustache ran to his chair in the living room to look out the window. Several shorter honks brought Jeffers and me to the front door.

"Hey," Paul said, his head sticking out the driver's side window of one of the smallest cars I'd ever seen.

It was a cherry-red Fiat 500.

"Whose is this?" I asked.

"A buddy of mine," he said, somehow extricating himself from behind the wheel. "I'm babysitting his dog for a few days and he left me the keys. Come on, we're going on an adventure."

"What?"

"I have food, an overnight bag, and a full tank. Get Moustache and let's go."

"Where?"

"It's a surprise! You're going into tech rehearsals next week, which means I'll hardly see you. So, to ensure that I don't forget what you look like during that time, I've planned a getaway."

Paul was right. I'd be teching two shows at the same time, which meant a series of twelve-hour days. This was easily our last chance for some quality time for a while.

I smiled. "Let me grab a few things."

"I've got everything you'll need," he said, giving Jeffers a wink.

Jeffers laughed. "Enjoy it now. Once you're married…"

I rolled my eyes at Jeffers and gave Paul a playful smack as he passed by me, picked up Moustache, and carried him to the car. Jeffers earned a further whack from my purse as I locked up.

I pulled open the passenger door and quite literally froze. Lying in the backseat was a full-grown St. Bernard and sitting atop the giant dog was Moustache. His eyes looked as if they would bulge out of his head. The two of us stared at each other, mouths agape.

"This is Tulip," Paul said, as if it were the most normal thing in the world. "She's a sweetie. Get in."

"We can't…" I stammered, "He can't…" I said, indicating Moustache.

"He'll be fine. Come on!"

I looked to Jeffers for support.

He crossed his arms and shrugged. Still laughing.

I took a deep breath, got in the car, and tried not to imagine the ruckus that would inevitably occur when Moustache came out of his catatonia.

Paul backed the car out of the driveway and Jeffers waved as if watching the *Queen Mary* depart. Realizing I still held the remains of his croissant, I rolled down the window and threw it at him, which only encouraged further theatrics.

"This isn't a good idea," I said when we'd turned the corner. "Moustache—"

"Moustache is fine. Look at him."

I turned in my seat to find Moustache curled up on Tulip's back and the two of them sound asleep.

He gave my knee a squeeze, and then he took my hand and brought it to his lips. "Everything's fine."

In Gratitude

When I wrote *Encore*, I dreamed of making Bella's story a series. I'm a fan of mystery series and there are several I follow. There is something wonderful about really getting to know characters—growing with them, rejoicing with them, and having your heart break right alongside them. It's what I wanted for Bella and Moustache and Jeffers, but I didn't know if I had it in me. I even balked when my first publisher wanted to put "A Bella James Mystery" on the cover as I felt that committed me to a sequel, at least, and I was afraid I wouldn't be able to deliver. After two years, I'm delighted to bring you *Triple Threat* and among my first acknowledgments, I have to thank you—each and every one of you who read *Encore* and expressed your wish for more. I was writing *Triple Threat* during a hard time in my life and it was your enthusiasm for *Encore* and your love of Bella (or Moustache—who am I kidding?) that pushed me forward.

There were several others who were instrumental in *Triple Threat's* fruition and who deserve equal thanks.

Over twenty years ago, Stephon Walker helped to lace up my medieval costume at a Renaissance Faire. We became friends, lost touch, reconnected years later, and when I learned he was working as a vet tech, he became my go-to for veterinary accuracy.

For medical accuracy, I'd like to thank Dr. Peter Collins, MD, FRCPC, who I've only had the pleasure of meeting via email and who treated my writing and the story with such care.

To capture the policing world, I had help from some of St. John's finest, who have asked that their names be withheld but who deserve the recognition all the same.

There are a few characters who you've met in this book whose personal and professional challenges are drawn from conversations I had with Lorne Gretsinger. I've been very lucky to have worked with Lorne for many years and to call him a friend, and I am grateful for his bravery in sharing his own experiences with me.

As with *Encore*, I thank Peter Millard for being my Shaw Festival expert. He is the dearest of friends, an exceptional actor, and 31-year veteran of the Festival.

I also had a wonderful army of test readers who slogged through the rough drafts with love: Deborah Drakeford, Danielle Irvine, Jill Kennedy, Mary Koetting, Michelle O'Connell, Phyllis DeRosa Koetting, and Barbara O'Keefe. Ladies, I am ever grateful.

As I am to Mary Ann Blair and the team at Iguana Books. I am so thrilled to be a part of their family.

And then there's *my* family, which is a little bit different from when I wrote *Encore*. I went through a divorce and I lost my dear dog, Grady, just two months before finishing *Triple Threat*. He left me with fourteen wonderful years of inspiration to draw from, and he continues to make me laugh through Moustache's antics.

I do not have enough words to reflect the kind of support I've received from my parents. *Unwavering*, *fervent*, and *heartening* are all good, but nowhere near sufficient. I feel *thanks* is insufficient as well, so I anxiously await the creation of a more accurate and encompassing word.

Thanks for reading, all. I'm already working on book three ☺.

About the Author

Alexis has been working as a professional actor on stage and screen for over twenty years. Her debut novel, *Encore*, received nominations for both an Arthur Ellis and Bony Blithe Award in 2016. Alexis lived in Niagara-on-the-Lake for ten years and currently makes her home in St. John's, Newfoundland, with a Bernedoodle puppy named Sebastian. She loves scary movies, dirty gin martinis, and has a terrible weakness for potato chips ☺.

CPSIA information can be obtained
at www.ICGtesting.com
Printed in the USA
LVOW12s1146200418
574184LV00001B/24/P